The Curious Vision of Sammy Levitt and Other Stories

Endowed by

Tom Watson Brown

and

The Watson-Brown Foundation, Inc.

The Curious Vision of Sammy Levitt

and Other Stories

Cliff Graubart

To June,
and to the love of books.
Cliff Graubart
12/8/12

MERCER UNIVERSITY PRESS
MACON, GEORGIA

MUP/ H857

© 2012 Mercer University Press
1400 Coleman Avenue
Macon, Georgia 31207
All rights reserved

First Edition

Books published by Mercer University Press are printed on acid-free paper that meets the requirements of the American National Standard for Information Sciences—Permanence of Paper for Printed Library Materials.

Mercer University Press is a member of Green Press Initiative (greenpressinitiative.org), a nonprofit organization working to help publishers and printers increase their use of recycled paper and decrease their use of fiber derived from endangered forests. This book is printed on recycled paper.

Library of Congress Cataloging-in-Publication Data

Graubart, Cliff.
The curious vision of Sammy Levitt and other stories / Cliff Graubart. -- 1st ed.
p. cm.
ISBN 978-0-88146-395-8 (hardback : alk. paper) -- ISBN 0-88146-395-7 (hardback : alk. paper) -- ISBN 978-0-88146-375-0 (e-book) -- ISBN 0-88146-375-2 (e-book)
1. Jews--United States--Fiction. 2. Short stories, Jewish. I. Title.
PS3607.R38C87 2012
813'.6--dc22
2012021583

Contents

*To Terry Kay who read it, then encouraged me,
and then forwarded it to Marc Jolley.
Thank you both.*

*To Dan Sklar who helped me realize I was close.
Thanks to Frank O. Smith and Liza Nelson.*

*To Pat Conroy, who changed my life.
I love you for it.*

*To my wife Cynthia, whom I love, and who
makes it all possible, and worthwhile.*

*To Anne Rivers Siddons and Heyward Siddons
for their constant love and support.*

To Rachel and Norman, I wrote this for you.

The Curious Vision of Sammy Levitt

1

Sammy looked at his watch. The iridescent numbers began their glow in the early evening shade, letting him know that it was four-twenty and reminding him of his bar mitzvah lesson in a few minutes. A pang hit him in the stomach, the same feeling he got every Sunday afternoon when the excitement and hope of Friday had dissolved into the fear of Monday and school.

Sammy didn't do well in school. He failed often and was embarrassed by his lack of performance. When he was called on in class he would stand up and stare at the teacher, unable to answer because he never really studied. He didn't know how to study, so he stood for what seemed like an eternity, as if scolded, shifting his weight from one leg to the other, looking up and down, resting his hands on the desk and then removing them so as not to appear disrespectful. He squinted his eyes in feigned thought sometimes, hoping that the teacher would allow him to sit before his eyes welled. Eventually she would, if she were gentle, and as he slowly slid back into his seat, he would blink his eyes furiously, hoping the tears could be garnered back and not roll down his cheeks.

Some of his darkest days were spent in P.S. 187 in uptown Manhattan. His heart would leap whenever a teacher apologized to the class for not having the exams graded. He wouldn't even make-believe he was disappointed like the rest of the class. His record was too well known. On that day he would get a reprieve—a day without being humiliated—a day without being asked his grade. But eventually the grades would come, and the students would eagerly question each other.

"What did you get, Sammy?"

"I failed," he would answer without even looking at his paper, hoping that he wouldn't have to explain. He was at an age when he didn't yet know that he didn't have to answer all questions posed.

Later, after the excitement had died down, after the class had resumed and had forgotten the test results, he would turn the page and see the angry graffiti—the red marks and strikeouts—and wonder if the teacher was mad at him. Often, when he was home after school playing a board game of baseball by himself and keeping records of the batting averages of his favorite players, he would imagine himself in a prison cell away from school and homework, where nothing was required of him, and where all that was important was that Reese or Robinson got on base.

Sammy rested the palm of his baseball glove on his knee as he looked toward the pitcher's mound from his position in leftfield. A kid rode by on a bicycle, snapping him out of a daydream. He had no idea how many outs there were. He scraped his foot nervously from side to side across the concrete, dislodging some dirt, and then he heard the crack of the stick. He looked up instinctively as he always did when the schoolyard became darker. One couldn't see the ball until it cleared the roof line and crossed what was left of a daylight sky, and if it was a line drive one couldn't see it at all. But the pitcher could, and he would shout coordinates.

"Deep, deep!"

But Sammy spotted the ball too late. It was not as high as it was long, and he had no chance. As he ran after it, he could hear the slam of a teammate's glove as it hit the concrete and as he yelled, "Shit!" in disgust at the batter rounding the bases. The game was over.

"Another one!" someone shouted. "Same sides."

"I can't," Sammy said. "I gotta go."

"Just one inning," someone pleaded.

"Can't."

The boys re-thought the time. It was darker now, not like when they started, when the ball could still be seen. Bats fluttered and dived in the corners of the schoolyard.

"I gotta go, too," another said, and suddenly three or four mouths sharing a sixteen-ounce Tops cola seemed more appealing. They sauntered out of the schoolyard, each carrying his glove. One bounced the ball a few feet ahead, putting a spin on it so that it bounced back to meet him the next step. Another snatched it and threw it against a "no-parking" sign as they headed for Stein's candy store on 187th Street, all the while talking baseball.

But Sammy was already distant. He could hear the first few bars of his haftorah in his head, that part of the Prophets he would have to sing on the morning of his bar mitzvah in front of the entire congregation. His haftorah was long, and there was a lot to memorize, but he liked to sing and could carry a tune. What he feared was singing in front of a crowd. He held on to the thought that singing was different from talking. It wouldn't be like being in front of the class in school. Here he would know the answers. He would be prepared. He had practiced for months, so he knew exactly what to say. The fact was, he liked singing so much that he sometimes imagined himself as a cantor when he grew up, especially after he saw *The Jazz Singer*, until he realized that being a cantor would require his presence in synagogue every day, and when he thought of that, he decided he would rather be in the prison cell with his board game. Becoming a bar mitzvah was teaching him a lot. For one thing he'd learned that this event was as much for his parents as it was for him. It seemed that lately all they talked about at home was his bar mitzvah. His father could speak of little else.

"In a few days you'll be the first boy to be bar-mitzvahed in the new shule. Did you know that?"

Oh, he knew it alright. While the rabbi was preparing the shule for its first bar mitzvah, Sammy was learning about another thing—pressure. He had never felt like this before, where people were counting on him for a real event. It wasn't like the immediate pressure in school to answer a question. This was more opaque, off in some vague but encroaching future.

He first felt the effects when he noticed a twitch in his nose occasionally. It had started just a few days before. He was sitting by the window overlooking Broadway, watching the cars go by and thinking about his haftorah. Then he felt a spasm roll across his nostril and bend his nose to one side. It twitched again and again. He went to the mirror to look, waited, and sure enough the strange feeling returned. He saw his nose jerk to the side and his mouth open at an angle, exposing his missing tooth. Nothing like this had ever happened to him before. It was ugly, but he thought that it would be like the hiccups and just stop, like hiccups of the face. But it didn't. He tried not to think about it. But then he would.

The Washington Heights Jewish Center rested on the crest of a hill near a subway station not far from the George Washington Bridge. On one side stood an old five-story walk-up and on the other, seemingly carved from the igneous rock upon which Upper Manhattan is built, sat a small newsstand with a green canvas awning that jutted out over the magazines and newspapers spilling toward the sidewalk. As Sammy passed, he saw old man Richter, the stand's manager, who rarely spoke. Sammy could see him in the winter rocking on each foot to keep warm, waiting for the sound of the next train coming into the station downstairs, and for his customers to exit. Then he might straighten the *World Telegram and Sun* or the *Journal American* and the more popular *Post*, the three evening papers. After that he might blow into his woolen gloves, their fingers cut off so he could better handle the papers and the change. Sammy eyed the *Daily Worker* on the newsstand shelves and wondered what it looked like inside. He'd always wanted to pick it up, but he never had for fear of being noticed.

Across the street was a small park about the size of a city block named for George Washington, because he had commanded troops from here during the Revolution with its strategic view of the Hudson River. Old men played chess on boards painted onto the slick tile surfaces of concrete tables. Children played on swings and monkey bars under watchful eyes. Directly across the park, facing the synagogue, was the entrance to Hudson View Gardens, an English Tudor apartment complex crowned with a heavy slate roof and covered with ivy climbing up its dark brick exterior. The sprawling three-story complex was built during the early 1920s, with a peaceful one-way street on its entrance side and a view of the Hudson on the other—that is, until after the war, when a group of apartments were constructed even closer to the river and cancelled its vista. Yet it was still the most desirable place to live in Washington Heights, with its private brick driveway guarded by a big, black cast-iron gate, and its small grocery in the basement.

The mythology in the neighborhood was that Jewish people were not welcome there, so when Sammy passed by, he would look through the windows to catch a glimpse of life inside. He wondered how Christians lived. He could see the molding near the ceiling from the sidewalk, and he held on to that image. "Christian molding," he thought, and then he would compare it to the molding at home, thinking that it must be different but not able to tell how, just accepting it because he couldn't live there. But this didn't bother him. His apartment was much closer to the schoolyard anyway. It didn't bother him that he was different. On many occasions he heard his parents discussing vacation plans, which usually meant trips upstate, though not to Lake Placid, which was off limits to them. It was like anything else in his life. If it didn't seem to bother his parents, it didn't bother him.

But he remembered a time that it did bother him. He was sitting in the back of the 1946 Plymouth with Manny, his older brother. His parents had paused in front of a lodge somewhere upstate. It was dark, and they were looking for a place to sleep. Manny was curled up with smelling salts in his nose to ease his car sickness, and Sammy was just resting, staring at the dome light as his parents looked at a map. He could see a "vacancy" sign blinking in front of a handsome white clapboard house. To him the inns all seemed to be operated by white-haired old ladies. He listened to his parents talking in Yiddish about whether to go in or try another. He didn't speak Yiddish, but he understood enough.

"It's late," his father said, getting out of the car to check the vacancy. His mother turned to check on the boys, and Sammy closed his eyes. A few minutes later, he saw his father come down the stairs and open the car door.

"The rooms are lousy," he said, driving off, but not at the same deliberate speed that Sammy was used to. Sammy knew he was angry, and he pretended to be asleep so as not to embarrass his dad. He knew the rooms weren't lousy. He imagined, one day, returning to those travel lodges and asking for a room and getting it because he didn't have an accent.

Sammy pulled open the new, heavy metal doors of the synagogue and walked down the hall. The marble floors cast a quiet sound, like the light tap one might hear in an office building, far different from the creaking wooden floors of the old shule he was used to, which rested under Kurtzman's candy store down the hill. He sat down along the wall across from the rabbi's office and waited for his lesson. The high pitch of Barry Levine's voice screeched out of the office. Sammy could picture the rabbi's face contorting as Barry missed more notes than he hit.

It was one thing to memorize your haftorah, but it was another to sing in tune. Levine had once asked Sammy how he sang in tune and he didn't know what to say. Sammy didn't feel like he had trained to be in tune. He just did. Levine was very popular in school. Being smart and a good athlete guaranteed it. So Sammy felt strange being better at something, a feeling he hadn't had since first arriving in Manhattan from Brooklyn, where he had learned to play punchball by using his fist instead of merely slapping the ball underhand, as they were doing in Washington Heights. Though he was short, he could hit a ball as far as the biggest kid in the class, ensuring him instant popularity. The advent of softball the next year as a recess activity, however, had put an end to that—his frame was too small to swing the bat as if it were a toy. He was fast and could play well, but at less than 100 pounds, he couldn't hit for distance no matter how hard he tried. Already he could see the forearms of some of his friends who were developing muscles, and he was envious of the veins that pressed against the skin of their arms. They were becoming men.

Across from where Sammy sat, a painter brushed a walnut stain across a new door to the rabbi's office. The door was made of different shades of pine, inviting paint to cover its differences. Recessed were four rectangular sections and two square sections above them. Blocking the sections to form the door were long strips of pine with shades varying from light pink to pale yellow and with a wide assortment of grains—some even as the desert sand, some with lines nearly straight, and one that looked like small, trailing waves coasting to shore. Sammy watched as the painter's brush eased its way down, deepening the lines in some cases, blending the shapes in others. Dividing the door horizontally were strips of pine connecting to the vertical sides and seemingly crisscrossing them.

The painter noticed Sammy watching now, and his strokes became more deliberate as if suddenly he took even greater pride in his work. Back and forth he followed with a rag in his free hand, catching the drips at the corners or simply wiping across the whole strip, removing the glare from the stain. It was the rabbi's door, so the painter was careful. Although he had run through the process on countless doors in the building, here he took his time.

Sammy sat by the wall, almost in a trance, staring at the raw pine as it slowly and methodically changed under the stain. As he watched, he hummed the first few bars again and again so that he wouldn't enter the rabbi's office cold, for he was still nervous. He hadn't even started writing his bar mitzvah speech—the speech that would tell the congregation and his entire family what it felt like to become a man in the eyes of God. He didn't know.

The painter placed the brush down and examined his work. He touched the top of the door to check for drying and stepped back, satisfied of his work. Leaving the door open, he placed a "wet paint" sign on the doorknob, checked his watch, and walked down the hall. The sign dangled from the doorknob at an angle and a corner touched the paint. Sammy stared at it and imagined it being stuck there the next morning.

It was a nice door, he thought—rich in color, much nicer than the brown painted metal doors of the old shule, which had dents all over them as if riddled with bullets that hadn't penetrated. No, these doors were classy, almost baronial by comparison. The stain made the grain of the wood stand out, and Sammy could see different shapes, shapes that reminded him of the shadows on the ceiling at home as he lay in bed and waited for sleep. He didn't see monsters in the ceiling, but he saw things, like "almost-a-car" and "almost-a-horse." Here in the shule he began to see the shape of a face. He tilted his head a bit. Yes, definitely a face, a man's face. He thought how neat it was that the stain could bring out these lines. In fact, the face reminded him of the many pictures he had seen of Jesus, like those he had just seen in *Life* magazine. There was the beard. He could definitely see a beard. And the long hair down to his shoulders, only the lines continued all the way down to the base of the door. The face was looking up like in many of the pictures he had seen before. He had large, owlish eyes and his hair seemed parted down the middle—that, too, continued on down—but it still looked like a face.

What a weird coincidence, Sammy thought, for the grain in the wood to somehow have "almost-a-face" in it. He wondered then, when everyone saw it, would the rabbi have it painted over, or would the congregation arrange to give it to the church down the street? The Christians ought to have it, he thought. If Moses' face were in the door, wouldn't the rabbi be thrilled? What a break for him! But who needs Jesus?

A silence filled the hall as Sammy realized that Barry had stopped singing. That meant he would be coming out soon. He heard the main door open down the hall and saw Gerry Friedman stumble in, dropping his book and accidentally kicking it down the slick marble floor.

"Shit," he said as he gained his balance, picked up his book, and sat down beside Sammy.

"Who's in there?" he asked.

"Levine, but I think he's finished."

"Did you study?" Gerry asked while opening his book.

"Nah," he said reflexively, and then, "A little."

"I didn't do shit."

Sammy believed him. Gerry was one of those kids who never studied and who never seemed to worry except on testing day and who still passed all his courses. To Sammy, it seemed that every word or thought in school was designed to make passing tests impossible. He was thankful for Melvin and Johnny, two kids who were left back once and were considered the dumbest. Sometimes he would look at them after an exam and feel relieved that he wasn't alone.

The rabbi's door opened, and out came Levine, with a fresh paint stain on his sleeve.

"How is he?" Gerry asked.

Barry rolled his eyes and kept on walking.

Gerry and Sammy looked at each other and laughed nervously. Gerry rubbed his eye with the palm of his hand, a habit he had when he was anxious. Sammy was relaxed and confident, an unusual feeling for him since, after all, this was considered "school" as well. He couldn't remember a time when he wasn't afraid of school. Still, his nose twitched.

The cherry wood of the rabbi's desk seemed pale under the harsh fluorescent light. Sammy was reminded of the blue lights his father intermixed with white in the fur market to give the skins a bluish cast to make them more appealing. Every shop had them, every dealer, every manufacturer, and every showroom. Sammy often wondered if there was a reaction from the customer when she emerged in daylight. Did she notice the difference? Why didn't anyone complain? Why didn't anyone ask to see the coat in the normal light?

The desk and the worn cloth on the armrest of the chair were the only pieces of furniture that remained from the old shule. Sammy missed the creaky wooden floors, the brown, hollow metal doors that banged but didn't click shut, the gobs of paint that kept them shiny but couldn't conceal the dents, and the initials carved into them. He missed the ring-a-levio games he played on the steps outside waiting for the class to begin. The boys chose sides based on their baseball allegiance. Sammy was a Dodgers fan and the Dodgers fans were always smaller in number than the Yankees fans, so the Giants and Dodgers would play against the Yankees. It was Manhattan and not Brooklyn, which explained part of it, but the Dodgers had Jackie Robinson and Cal Abrams, the only Jewish ballplayer in the city. So Sammy wondered why more neighborhood kids weren't Dodgers fans. But the Yankees always seemed to win. And kids love winners.

The new synagogue, with its expanded facilities, brought new faces, and Sammy already felt like an outsider. Not that it really mattered, since after his bar mitzvah he would be finished with Hebrew school and could be called to serve in a minyan every morning if needed. Having the ten men necessary to form a minyan wasn't always a guarantee. Images of one of his friends being summoned off the street on a Saturday morning on his way to the schoolyard with stick and baseball glove in hand, begging an old-timer not to ask him, and then pleading that he wasn't thirteen while his buddies laughed, made Sammy tense until he realized that he wasn't big like Haselbauer and wouldn't be recognized as old enough. But if he were asked, he knew how he would handle it.

"Hey, boychick," an old-timer might yell. "You bar-mitzvahed—no?"

"No," he would answer.

"Didn't I see you bar-mitzvahed?" the old man might ask, bluffing.

"Not yet. Next year," he would answer, winning this early game of wits and thereby ensuring his stickball game would not be pre-empted by prayer.

The rabbi was standing behind his desk, piled high with papers and unopened mail. An "in-and-out" box had long ago lost its purpose. Just a few weeks before, the room had been bare. The rabbi marveled at how much time he needed just to read his daily mail. He needed help, but then struggles with the executive committee arose, and he'd forgotten about mail. Later he set aside some time just to straighten his desk, forgot that, too, and instead spent the time shifting papers looking for his pipe cleaners.

Behind the rabbi's desk, lining the unfinished cinderblock wall was a gray metal shelf that held some of his books, all leaning to the side and wanting bookends. He laid books at the end to act as a stop but they were losing their grip. Many others sat on the floor in stacks and in boxes, along with framed pictures and diplomas. Chalk dust spotted the rabbi's black suit, which was shiny from too many cleanings.

A teacher who loved discussion, he longed for the challenging days at Yeshiva University before the war, when every student seemed to have an opinion on the formation of the state of Israel. His hurried walk to the blackboard to illustrate a point brought chuckles to the class and spread chalk dust everywhere, including on his face as he placed his chin in the palm of his hand, listening intently to his students. The suit reminded Sammy of Miss Barr, his first-grade teacher. She was born at the end of the last century and possessed skills and attitudes honed from that time. She wore only black dresses and never smiled. Sammy feared her most when he was late. He would walk into class holding Manny's hand, looking upward at what, to him, was a giant with a bun of gray-black hair, and would wait for her to scold his older brother. He didn't remember why they were late, and he always vowed not to be late the next day, but he always forgot. Every morning Manny would tell him to "Hurry up, we're gonna be late!" And every morning he thought he was hurrying, but still, sometimes they would be late. Manny never blamed him, though, and told him not to worry when he bent down to take off Sammy's coat after the scolding.

"A-ha!" the rabbi exclaimed in victory, as he located his pipe cleaner behind a stack of papers.

"Okay, Sammy, you begin."

"Where, Rabbi?"

"From where we left off," the rabbi answered. Sammy began and the rabbi began as well, humming to himself as he cleaned his pipe.

The sound of a match being struck caused Sammy to hesitate. The rabbi sang Sammy's bars to help him, thinking that Sammy was stuck. Sammy continued, and the rabbi nodded in agreement. As Sammy sang he noticed Gerry writing something. Gerry saw him and pointed with his pen to the page. But Sammy didn't want to look. Gerry was always kidding around, and Sammy didn't want trouble. His record at Hebrew school was not stellar.

"AAAAAAAAAAHHHHHH," Sammy continued, the rabbi humming along as he picked up a letter opener. SLASH. A letter ripped open, and Sammy hesitated. The rabbi continued for him loudly so Sammy could pick it up, not realizing that his opening of the envelope was the cause of the hesitation. "AAAAAAAAHHHH," Sammy repeated and continued. SLASH. Another envelope, but this time Sammy pressed on. "AAAHHHHHH." SLASH. "AAAHHH." SLASH. It began to sound like a symphony.

"Good, good," the rabbi exclaimed, reading his mail and nodding his head to Sammy's chant. From the corner of his eye,

Sammy could see Gerry shaking, suppressing laughter. It was then that Sammy smelled it. Sulfur.

Someone had farted. Then Gerry moved his note closer to Sammy and bent down to tie his shoe to conceal his laughter. The rabbi, still involved with his mail, did not raise his eyes. Sammy glanced at the note: "Something must have crawled up the rabbi's ass and died." By now, the new smell of rotting eggs was slowly overtaking any odor that remained of the tobacco. Sammy knew immediately that he had made a mistake. He never should have looked at that note.

Gerry was still tying his shoe, unable to rise, tears of laughter hitting the floor. He began making noises. Sammy hoped that the rabbi would light another match and reclaim the room for tobacco, but then he imagined the room exploding into flames and began to laugh. He coughed, trying to cover it and still trying to sing his haftorah. He stopped for a second, closed his eyes, and took a breath. He tried to think about something extremely serious, employing every ounce of concentration to counter the mood. But it was no use. This was one of those times when laughing at the wrong thing, in the wrong place, made it ten times funnier. He was finished. He let out some air and with it came another laugh. Then he tried covering it with a fake sneeze. This caused Gerry to lose control and they both sat there, unable to stop laughing, their bodies shaking furiously but silently.

The rabbi, realizing that Sammy's singing had stopped, looked up, surveyed the situation, and slammed his fist on his desk, knocking off a group of papers and creating even more laughter in the room.

"Stop!" he shouted. "What's so funny here?"

There was no answer.

"Did I miss a joke? Well?" he demanded.

Sammy composed himself and replied, "No, Rabbi."

"So?"

Each second seemed like an hour. What could Sammy tell him? That he'd farted? As if the rabbi hadn't known? I'm surprised the paint isn't peeling, Sammy thought.

"GET OUT! GET OUT!" the rabbi shouted. He waved his hand at them and they picked up their things and started for the door. As they closed the door behind them and passed by the secretary's desk, they heard a shout. "Come back here!"

"Oh, shit," Gerry said, as they stopped and turned back toward the room.

"Sit down," the rabbi commanded angrily, not willing to let them go home early. "Open your books and study," he said, annoyed, and walked out.

"Study what?" Sammy wanted to ask. The boys sat, but after a while they began giggling again.

"Wha'dya think he's doing?" Gerry asked during a break in the laughter.

Sammy shrugged. "I hope he's taking a shit." And then they started laughing again. They heard some noise outside and quickly straightened

"Cool it," Gerry said just as the rabbi opened the door.

"You know it won't be so funny if you're not prepared," he said. "You've both invested lots of time and energy, and it would be a shame if your parents didn't get to see you in front of the congregation. You haven't written your speeches yet, have you?" Sammy looked at Gerry and then back to the rabbi and shook his head. "Do you know what to say, Sammy? Do you have any idea what it means to be bar-mitzvahed?"

"No, Rabbi," he answered, thinking that the rabbi wasn't so angry anymore.

"What about you, Gerry? Do you know what it means to be Jewish?"

Gerry looked at the rabbi with a calm and blank expression. The rabbi turned his gaze on Sammy, implying the same question, and Sammy realized that he was speechless. He thought a second about his parents and his brother. His mind raced to his aunts and uncles. And then to dressing up for Rosh Hashanah and Yom Kippur. Then to the stories his father told him of the old country.

"Well?" the rabbi pressed.

"Different?" Sammy answered, with no clear idea what he meant. The rabbi looked surprised and pleased.

"Different?" the rabbi continued. "Chinese are 'different.'"

"Maybe not different," Sammy hesitated. He thought for a second. "Special," he said, enthused.

"Special's okay, but everybody's special. Go on," the rabbi said, opening his hands to encourage him.

"We're different. We go to shule on Saturdays and believe in different things." Sammy was delighted that he had hit on a word that worked.

"The Seventh-Day Adventists go to church on Saturday. So is that good or bad?"

Sammy thought for a second. "Just different. I mean special, good. It's good. It's just the way it is."

"Do you like that Sammy, or does it make you uncomfortable?"

"I don't know. It's okay. Sometimes it's uncomfortable. Sometimes I'm afraid."

"When?"

"Around Broadway."

The rabbi smiled. "Why Broadway?"

"Things happen there," Sammy said. "Well, once something happened there." He began to relate the story of when he, Shelley, and Dickie Meyer were returning from a movie at the

Loews theater at 175th and Broadway. Two kids, two Irish kids, about the same age, were following them down Broadway.

"I think they're Jew boys," was what one of them said to his friend in mock conversation.

"Yeah, I think you're right. They look like faggots."

Sammy remembered wondering if they could outrun the two kids. Dickie was very fast and Sammy was okay, but Shelley couldn't run at all. The kids would stomp him. Dickie was taller than Sammy and Shelley—and stronger. They continued walking, pretending that they hadn't heard anything, hoping the kids would go away. And then they heard it again.

"They must be deaf. Hey, Jew boys, you're in my way."

Sammy moved to the right, hoping to appease them, and Shelley and Dickie followed, causing the two kids behind them to laugh.

"You're still in my way."

Dickie turned. "C'mon, leave us alone," he said. Sammy turned, too, and gave a weak smile, his heart pounding. The two kids weren't big at all—about the same size, with no menacing scars—and yet they seemed to hold all the cards. Dickie turned back, not waiting for an answer, and kept walking, leading Sammy and Shelley.

"Leave us alone," one of the Irish kids sneered.

Sammy wished they were three or four blocks closer to home, maybe on Fort Washington Avenue where they would feel safer. Then one of them grabbed Dickie's arm and twisted it so hard he had to bend over as he walked.

"C'mon, let him go," Sammy pleaded.

"Shut up, pussy."

Sammy turned around and kept walking, seeking the faces of passers-by for help, but most were women with shopping strollers. No one seemed to notice. If they did, they probably just thought it was a case of "kids being kids." The five of them turned the corner and headed for Fort Washington Avenue, and Sammy felt lifted as they passed the Harlem Savings Bank, to which he and his dad would walk on some Friday nights. A glass frame held a big sign advertising one-percent interest. Dickie bent over more now, grunting as the kid applied more pressure.

"Are you alright?" Sammy asked. "You're hurting him," he said.

The kid smacked Sammy on the back of the head. "No shit, Sherlock." And then the two attackers laughed but still headed for Fort Washington Avenue. By now they were very confident, as there was no resistance at all. They passed the record store and the food store and wound up at the corner of Fort Washington and 181st Street. Sammy saw a cop across the street in front of the candy store and wondered how to call him, but he was afraid. Shelley saw him, too, and looked at him with the same question in his eyes. Sammy blinked his eyes to let Shelley know that he knew but still didn't know how to act.

They stood there for a moment before the boys let Dickie's arm go. Dickie straightened up and felt his arm but said nothing. The two boys turned, giving them the finger and then heading south down Fort Washington Avenue towards the bridge, not looking back once, as if brushing off a fly.

"Are you okay, Dickie?" Shelley asked.

"Yeah, I'm alright."

They walked home silently. Mostly what Sammy felt was relief. The thought of fighting the two boys had never entered his mind. Only escape. If he wished for anything then, it wasn't to be strong enough or brave enough to overpower his opponents but simply to disappear.

The rabbi took a drag on his pipe, realized it had gone out, and placed it on the desk. Just a hint of tobacco lingered. He walked around to his seat and sat rocking a bit against the backrest that gave easily to his large frame.

"Well, that is scary, Sammy. But that could happen anywhere. Granted, it is more likely to happen on Broadway near the Loews theater than in Fort Tryon Park. You know Yeshiva University is also on 181st Street, Sammy. Did you know that?"

Sammy lit up. "Yeah."

"You know, Sammy, maybe you should explore your feelings a little more about what it means to you to be Jewish and incorporate that into your speech. Being the first boy to be bar-mitzvahed in the new shule is an honor, and a lot of people will be in attendance besides your family. I would personally want to give it my best shot."

Sammy nodded. For the first time, he felt energy toward writing it. Then his nose twitched, and the rabbi looked at him. "I will," Sammy blurted out, hoping the rabbi hadn't noticed the twitch.

Later, as Sammy headed home for dinner, he reflected on the words of the rabbi, a man he had thought of only in fear or in jest. Hebrew school wasn't real school to him, and it played to a different standard. Nobody seemed to fail. But he would write a speech, he thought. Manny would help him. He felt serious about the speech, and he felt good about feeling serious. He would do well in school and that felt good.

2

Only one thing connected Sammy to Matt Margolis. At one time in their young lives, they both had been ostracized by the mothers of the neighborhood. When Sammy arrived from Brooklyn, he came armed with a vocabulary not according to Webster and bearing a library of pornographic comic books. Indeed, Brooklyn was more advanced than the sleepy, upscale neighborhood of Washington Heights in 1951. Sammy had loaned one of these comics to his friend Jeffrey, who saw fit to peruse this book surreptitiously on his lap at the dinner table. It didn't take a genius to discover why little Jeffrey, while glancing at pictures of a naked Superman plowing his way through America, was only pecking away at his food. Even now Sammy could remember asking Jeffrey at school, after Jeffrey's parents had read the riot act to Sammy's parents, "How can you be so stupid and yet live?" But the damage had been done. The word was out that a cancer had come to this yet undiscovered part of Washington Heights, and its name was "Sammy Levitt." By now, however, the incident had largely been forgotten. Sammy's father had made him throw his comics in the incinerator and cut off his thirty-five-cent-per-week allowance for a while, and Sammy had restricted his cursing to his peers.

Matt's cause celebre was more hands-on. He'd been caught instructing a few of his classmates how to masturbate. The class was held on the roof of 720 Fort Washington Avenue and was noticed by a lady hanging her wash on top of the 700 building. Sammy, thankfully, had not registered for that class or he most assuredly would have been banished. No, it was four other lucky youngsters who were caught pants down, penis in hand and a Vargas picture on the ground splattered with semen.

Matt's tutorial on the fine art of beating one's meat had earned him the contempt of every adult who learned of it, but he wouldn't have been taken to the police station had it not been for the policeman who came to investigate the incident. The policeman was Chinese, and Matt had never seen a Chinese policeman. When he arrived on the scene, the first words out of the policeman's mouth were, "What have you got there?"

Matt, rising from a bent over position, half in pain and half in ecstasy, holding on to a slowly declining penis, looked at the policeman in amazement. Before he could think, he blurted out, "My shrong!" The kids howled. With his pants still down around his ankles, Matt was dragged by the ear down the stairs, all to a chorus of laughter behind him. The event would earn him the first of three juvenile delinquency cards.

That Matt would get into trouble like this seemed odd, for he was one of only a few kids in the whole neighborhood who went to a private school. They were a different breed. For one thing, Matt lived in apartments along the K-line. Sammy's T-line apartment had two bedrooms, but the K-line apartments had three, along with a sunken living room and two bathrooms. People who lived on the K-line were considered well-off. Even Matt's mother didn't look like other mothers. She was beautiful. Whenever she left the building, she looked, the way she dressed, as if she were shuttling off to a screen test. Sammy couldn't remember seeing her carrying groceries.

The kids who went to private school dressed alike, and Sammy admired their clothes. They were the only kids who wore loafers, and button-down plaid and oxford shirts, and pressed chinos. He wondered where they got these clothes. His mother bought his clothes from Klein's, a bargain basement. He could see his mother laying out clothes she had bought, clothes that he liked, but they weren't anything like those worn by the private-school kids. Sometimes, when he was downtown scouting for old *Sport* magazines on 14th Street, he would see what was obviously a class visiting from Westchester or someplace outside of the city, and they were all dressed in loafers—even the girls. Like a lofty army of pawns, they walked through the city with a confidence he admired, though it seemed strange to him that they were gawking at the sites he knew so well and was so comfortable with, yet they lived only a few miles away.

The next day, after what was to be known as the rabbi's "Great Fart," the weather was exceptionally cool. When Sammy arrived at the schoolyard glove in hand, he was surprised to see a few one-on-one basketball games going and kids throwing footballs. In the city, the schoolyard activity was like nature itself and changed with the season. He could put his stick away for the rest of the winter. His favorite sport was over for now. He didn't feel like playing football yet. The World Series was still on. So he turned and headed for home. It was Thursday, the last day in the week for Hebrew school, and he could practice his haftorah, something he never did until he reached class.

As he walked near the park, he was struck by something odd. Among the bits of trash that coat the streets and sidewalks of New York, he noticed a line of peanuts that stretched for what looked like ten feet. But these were not the usual peanut shells and skins one might find mixed with fallen leaves, dirt, and acorns. This was an autobahn headed around the corner of the entrance to the park. Sammy stopped, amused by the spectacle of a pigeon nibbling on a peanut, looking up for danger, moving down again, and progressing toward the entrance. Another pigeon landed a step ahead of the first one and they began jockeying around each other to get to the next peanut first.

Finally one of the pigeons snatched the last peanut before the curve, gulped it, looked up, turned the corner, and disappeared from view. Then Sammy heard a loud scream. He made a cautious wide turn to discover a gleaming Matt Margolis holding the pigeon under his windbreaker. He looked up, bursting with success.

"I got him!"

"What are you gonna do with it?" Sammy asked.

Matt thought for a second. "I don't know. Keep him for a while." Sammy immediately imagined himself bringing a pigeon into the house and his mother's reaction.

"Matt," Sammy said, "they have a disease."

"What kind of disease?"

"How do I know? They just do. Ask anybody." Matt looked around as if that were really an option.

"You better watch out for the park, man," Sammy warned.

"Yeah, you're right."

"You're amazing, Matt, really amazing," Sammy said, but wasn't sure why. Matt remained stationary, still hovering over the squirming pigeon.

"I bet he's shitting all over your jacket," Sammy said. Matt slowly opened one side of the coat and peeked inside. Sensing an opening on the other side, the pigeon took full advantage, scrambling out and then flying away.

"Shit. Look what you made me do."

"What'd I do?"

"Shit," Matt said, as he rose. Then, as if they had just seen each other that day for the first time, Matt asked Sammy if he wanted to play Fox and Hounds. But Sammy told him that he had to go to Hebrew school soon. "How about cards? You wanna flip?" Sammy touched his rear pocket to see whether he'd brought his cards. He had.

"Okay," Sammy said. "But only for a few minutes. I gotta go, really."

"That's okay," Matt answered, delighted. Sammy took out his shooter, a Wayne Terwilliger card he didn't value. It was lined with Scotch tape on all sides and felt nice and solid to the touch. He had five or six cards in his pocket he was willing to lose, along with a Curt Simmons he wasn't but needed to show to lure interest.

"What'dya got?" Sammy asked. Matt took out about double that amount and laid out, among other things, a Minnie Minoso and a Pee Wee Reese. Sammy didn't think that Matt was a Dodgers fan, so he thought he might not value that one too highly. They walked to a spot with less foot traffic and cleared a space of leaves and small stones. "Flip or shoot?" Sammy asked.

"Shoot."

"I'll flip you for who shoots first." Sammy placed his shooting card between his middle finger and thumb and gently flipped it over. "Call it," he instructed as the card floated down, flipping over and over.

"Heads!" Matt shouted. It was heads.

Sammy took his Terwilliger card and practiced his moves while Matt got ready. Matt took out his card, knelt down, and sent his shooter sailing. It fell hard against the wall, bounced off, and returned a few inches. Sammy knelt, moved his wrist back and forth, simulating a shot, and then let go. The card sailed gently and dropped before the wall, passing Matt's.

"I win," Sammy said. Matt flipped through his stash, pulled out a Dell Crandall, and gave it to Sammy. Back and forth it went like this, Sammy winning a few, and Matt winning a few. After a while Sammy looked at his watch. It was getting late. "I gotta go soon," he said.

"Just a few more." Matt shot again. This time he shot a leaner, one that leans against the wall and beats all others unless another card leans on top of it. Sammy had been sure he'd be going to Hebrew school with Pee Wee Reese in his pocket when the game had started, but he now found himself two cards in the hole.

"What's Hebrew school like?" Matt asked. Sammy was surprised because Matt was Jewish and should have known.

"It's alright. You study Jewish stuff. You know, for your bar mitzvah."

"Oh."

"Do your parents go to shule?"

"Nah. My parents are atheists."

Sammy's eyes widened. He remembered that Matt's parents were American-born and went to college. He thought how lucky Matt was. No haftorah. No shule.

"I gotta go, really."

"Aw, just a few more," Matt said pleading.

"I will if you give up Reese if you lose the next one. I'll shoot Curt Simmons, and you shoot Pee Wee." Sammy considered it odd that Matt even had baseball cards. He never played ball, never played with the kids in the neighborhood, and you never saw him in the schoolyard. He thought he must have played outside the neighborhood with friends from his school.

Matt thought for a moment. He flipped through his cards matter-of-factly and then looked at Sammy to see his reaction after stopping at the Pee Wee Reese card. Sammy stared at it, already imagining it in his stack so he could add it to his "keepers." "Okay," Matt finally answered.

Sammy took out his Curt Simmons card, flexed it, kissed it, and sent it sailing toward the wall. It landed and bounced off the wall, just a bit. It was a very good shot. Matt knelt down, flexed his wrist a few times, and followed with an equally fine shot that sailed through the air, finally hitting the wall but a bit more softly, hardly ricocheting at all and landing a hair closer to the wall. Matt had won.

Sammy stood frozen, staring at the cards as if he had just witnessed a miracle, then he watched Matt scoop up the cards and walk back beaming. Sammy blinked and opened his mouth. Nothing came out. Matt picked up his windbreaker, shook off the peanut shells, and put it on. Neither of them said a word for a moment as Matt stifled any joy.

"Another one?" Matt asked.

Sammy said nothing. He couldn't believe that he had lost. It was like that time he had lost a race in the schoolyard against Larry Krantz, who was bigger than he, but was heavy. He couldn't believe a big kid could run that fast. "Nah, I gotta go," he finally said, snapping out of it. He turned to leave. "See ya," he said.

And Matt returned the salutation. Sammy walked a few steps and then heard Matt call, "Sammy, here!" Sammy stopped, turned. Matt stood by the park entrance with a baseball card in his hand.

"What?" Sammy returned, almost in a pout.

"Here!" Matt repeated, this time waving his wrist for emphasis. "You can have it." Sammy walked back, thinking that Matt was returning his Curt Simmons card, and a warm feeling came over him. "You can have them, Sammy," Matt said. Sammy looked at Matt's hand. Matt was holding not only the Simmons card but the Pee Wee Reese card. Sammy looked at Matt. Matt stretched out his arm a bit farther, smiling now. "It's okay," he said. And Sammy took the cards gently.

"Thanks," Sammy said softly and turned away. He walked a few feet and then turned back. Matt had taken the peanuts out of his pocket and had begun to feed the pigeons again. "See ya!"

Sammy shouted. Matt looked up and waved, not wanting to shout so as not to scare the pigeons. Sammy continued towards Hebrew school, looked back again, and saw Matt in a pool of pigeons, now emptying the bag over the birds.

When he arrived in front of the shule, he saw a couple of kids flipping through baseball cards, comparing: "Got it, got it, don' got it, got it, got it, don' got it, don' got it, don' want it, got it..." He thought about Matt, pictured him standing by the park entrance stretching his arm out with the cards, and he felt tired. He wished he had not shot the last round, wished that Matt had not won his new baseball card. And as he looked at the smiling face of Pee Wee Reese, he thought about telling Matt how much he appreciated it, and then he placed it in his pocket. It was time for Hebrew school.

The finish on the door to the rabbi's office was dry, and the "wet paint" sign had been removed. Sammy looked at the face that reminded him of Jesus and walked inside.

3

Sammy looked far ahead to the exit of the subway station, past his apartment building, searching for his dad's gray Stetson hat. A few faces smiled, recognizing him. The grip of fall was on the subway-goers, a crisp wind at their back, heads bent down, one hand on the tip of each hat, the other firmly grasping a newspaper tucked under the arm.

"How's my boychick?" Sammy's father, Sid, asked, popping out of the crowd. He bent to give Sammy a kiss.

"Good," Sammy replied as he grabbed his father's hand and headed toward 720.

At the steps, he let go, skipped two at a time, and landed on the address numbers embedded on the white and green rubber mat. Over the years the white of the numbers had blended into the green so that they were losing their pristine quality, much as the building itself.

Mara Levitt stopped what she was doing in the kitchen when the door opened and wiped her hands on her apron.

Sid greeted his wife, took off his hat, and placed it on the top shelf of the hall closet. Then he walked to the foyer, fixed about an inch of scotch in a glass, and walked back to the kitchen. Meanwhile, Mara was admiring the meal she'd just made, sampling the chopped liver that sat on a leaf of lettuce in front of each table setting.

"So," Sid began as he gulped the shot down and placed the glass on the table, "any news?"

"Sonya called, and we're invited for dinner next week."

"What's the occasion?"

"Alan is coming home from the Army, and she wants to do something nice."

"Already? It seems like he went in yesterday."

"Yeah, I know," she answered as she gave Sid a spoonful of chopped liver to taste.

"Good," he said, complimenting her.

Sammy sauntered in and opened the refrigerator door.

"I'm hungry," he whined.

Sid placed his hands on the sides of Sammy's head and turned it playfully toward the kitchen table.

"A-ha!" he said. "Magic."

"Chopped liver!" Sammy shouted, and sat down to eat before anyone. Mara, his mother, looked at him and smiled. Then Manny came in, kissed Sid, and went to the refrigerator and pulled out a beer.

"Want one, Dad?"

"Sure."

They sat at the table.

"So, how's my Jerry Lewis?" Sid asked of Manny.

Manny shook his head in disgust.

"Not Jerry Lewis, Dad. Mort Sahl. He's more intellectual."

Sid opened his mouth in mock revelation. "Mort Sole, intellectual. How did I miss that?"

"'Sahl,' not 'Sole,'" Manny said defensively.

"Has Mr. Sahl been on the 'Ed Sullivan Show'?"

"As a matter of fact, he has," Manny said victoriously.

"He's funny," Sammy said.

"You don't even understand him," Manny said.

"Do, too," Sammy insisted.

"Alright, alright. Everyone understands him and he's a riot," Mara said to end it.

"So you still haven't answered my question," said Sid. "How are you doing?"

"In school?" Manny asked.

"School and your comedy act."

Sammy tried not to talk, so as not to break the rhythm of the conversation. It seemed to him that his father and brother knew the answers to big questions, and he didn't want to interrupt. Manny was nineteen now and wasn't around the house much, with college and the comedy act he was trying to develop, and Sammy missed him. Without him, the house was quiet.

"School's okay," Manny answered, "and my act is ready, I think. I still have to refine some stuff, but I have a gig at a fraternity party at school."

"A gig?" Sid asked.

"A job," Manny answered smiling. "Yeah, I gotta work on that tonight."

Sammy thought about school and felt his body slip. He had math homework he couldn't do.

"Manny, can you help me with my homework first?"

Manny gave a sigh as if caught. "How much? What kind?"

Sammy blurted out an answer with hope: "Math, not much."

Sid and Mara looked at Manny. The last time Sid had tried to help Sammy was with adding and subtracting fractions. Everything had changed since he was a kid in Poland. "Manny," Mara said, "when you needed help, Daddy was there to help you."

Manny looked at his father and smiled. "You mean this daddy?" he asked.

Sid ruffled Manny's hair and laughed. "Wise guy," he said.

"Yeah, I'll help you, Sammy. But we've got to hurry. My audience is very demanding."

Mara rolled her eyes and smiled.

As they were about to rise from dinner, the doorbell rang. Manny began barking like a dog. He rose and walked to the door, then growled softly but audibly. Sammy laughed.

"What are you doing?" Sid asked.

Manny put his finger to his lips and quietly opened the peephole to see who was there. Then he barked again. "Back, King!" he shouted. "Go on, boy!" Manny poked his head back into the dining room. "I got this," he whispered to his parents, who simply stared at him.

"It's okay," he continued, returning to the door. Again, he barked. "Back!" he said. Then he opened the peephole again. "Who is it?" he asked in a light and friendly voice.

"I'm Charles Ward, and this is Medina, my wife," a man answered.

"What can I do for you?" Manny asked.

"Do you know God's plan for your life?"

"Grrrrr!" growled Manny, imitating a dog. "Just a minute while I put up the dog. C'mon, King, c'mon."

Sammy laughed as he explained to his parents what Manny was doing.

"Crazy," Mara said as she rose to clear the table.

"What was that?" Manny asked through the door.

"Do you know God's plan for your life?" the man asked again.

"Haven't a clue," Manny said, then unlatched the door and opened it. Standing there was a couple—a white woman with a black man. They were dressed impeccably, she with a floral hat with too much fruit on top, and the man in a black-and-white-striped suit and wearing brown and white wing-tip shoes.

"God has a plan. It's all here," the man said, holding a pamphlet up to Manny. "Do you have the love of the Lord in your heart?" he continued.

Manny turned a bit and pointed to a mezuzah on the doorjamb.

"Do you know what that is? We're Jewish."

"You know, sir, we have the same Bible," the man's wife added quietly.

Manny smiled. "Terrific, then why are you here?" But before she or her husband could answer, Manny opened the door wide and said with a smile, "Ya know, why don't you both come on in?"

The man looked at his wife, and she smiled politely. Manny led them past the kitchen where Sid and Sammy sat transfixed. They'd never had any kind of "salespeople" enter their home. Usually Sid yelled, "We don't want any! Goodbye!" And that was that. The door was as far as they ever got, unless it was the egg man.

Manny ushered the couple past the dining room and into the living room. The man looked around cautiously. Sammy walked behind them and then turned off to his bedroom.

"Is the dog alright?" the man asked.

"No sweat," Manny said, waving the question away.

"Here, sit down, please," Manny said, pointing to the couch. The man's legs were thin and when he sat, they looked like stilts because of the sharp crease in his pant leg. Sammy's heart raced with anticipation. Then he began barking from his room.

"Don't worry," Manny said, back-stepping toward the room. Once inside, he grabbed Sammy and whispered, "You little shit. Cool it." He was smiling. Sammy nodded his head, trying to control his laughter.

"Stay!" Manny shouted and closed the bedroom door.

"Sorry about that," he said as he returned to the living room. "Don't worry, he's harmless." Sid walked from the kitchen, looked toward Manny, smiled weakly, and went into his bedroom and closed the door. Manny could hear his mother washing the dishes.

"So, you are here to tell me about 'the Word,' right?" Manny asked. Mr. Ward was reaching into his briefcase. "I know what you have there…'Flashlight,' 'Searchlight,' whatever. Right?"

"Let me ask you something," Manny continued. "What possessed you to knock on my door?" Mr. Ward looked at Manny blankly. "Can you tell me that?"

"What is it you want to accomplish? Wait, wait," Manny said, waving his hands as if to stop a game. "Let me see, you knocked on my door…," Manny's voice slowed deliberately. "And you didn't know me, and you said to yourself, 'Hey! Why don't we knock on this door and see if we can change this guy's religion? That sounds like a great idea. I don't know what his religion is, but let's change it.' Or…'Look! A mezuzah, a Jew. Let's change him into a Christian.' So I'm eating my dinner, and while I'm eating a matzo ball, you're outside thinking of ways for me to give up matzo balls and instead eat pork rinds. What a great idea! Ya know, it seems that for all my—"

"Well," Mr. Ward began, shifting and inching forward, "quite frankly, it is my mission. Our mission," he said, pointing to his wife, "to give the Word, the message of Jesus."

"Did you get this in a dream? Or was it in another way? You guys get visions, don't you? You see things? Or was it a dream? 'Good evening, Charlie. When you wake, you will change people's ideas on God.' Is that a typical dream? And you think that's a super idea? After a hard day at work you come home, eat dinner, and instead of sitting down with the paper, watching a little TV, or taking a walk in the park, you put on a suit and convert Jews? Wow! It doesn't get any better than that. If I had someone whisper in my ear while I was sleeping, asking me to wake up and convert people, that would be what is commonly called a nightmare! Instead of maybe watching a ballgame, or going out on a date, or minding my own business, I could go out and convert people. Why didn't I think of that?"

Sid came to the entrance of the living room and stayed back as Manny continued. "Let me ask you something. Did you ever convert anybody? I never heard of a soul converting in this neighborhood. Just once, did someone say, 'Wow, what a great idea! You turned me around. I could become a Christian, and instead of minding my own business, I can now mind somebody else's business, and tell them how they are going to hell unless they think just like me'? Gosh! I bet you haven't converted anyone. Or at least not many, and that makes you, what I would call, a lousy salesman. I hope you're not on commission."

"Manny, that's enough," Sid injected in a serious tone. Manny didn't turn to him, but he seemed to get the message. The Wards got up slowly. Mrs. Ward straightened her dress.

"I'm very sorry to have bothered you," Mr. Ward said, shaken. He looked to his wife, and she moved toward him as he began inching from behind the coffee table. He had never encountered such an evening. He had been ridiculed, shouted at, and probably hit by someone, but this was different. Manny walked ahead and unlocked the door, then pulled it open.

"I'm sorry, too," Manny said.

"God bless you," said Mrs. Ward, and let the door close behind her. Sid walked over to Manny and placed a hand on his shoulder.

"That was pretty awful, don't you think?" Sid asked.

Manny turned around. "Actually, I've always wanted to do that, Dad. It just pisses me off. But now I feel like crap. Those two people are probably very nice. God knows they have enough problems as it is. Why do they do it?"

"God only knows. But you were very hard on those two."

"Christ, what a pain in the ass."

"Christ has nothing to do with it. Besides, your brother needs you for his homework."

"Oh, geez."

"Manny! Please, I can't help here."

Manny placed his hand on Sid's shoulder now, almost looking down on him. "Only a miracle can help us here."

Manny stood behind Sammy, seated at his desk, as he flipped through his textbook for the right page.

"There. This page," Sammy said, as he pointed to the geometry problems.

"All of that? It'll take a year," Manny said, his voice rising.

"No, it won't," Sammy said pleading.

"Jesus Christ, let's go already."

They worked through three problems over the next half hour, until Sammy had an idea.

"One more, Manny. The last one." Manny looked at the problem: how to find the area of a triangle.

"Alright, this is what you do," Manny told him. "First, you have to figure out what this triangle would look like inside of a rectangle so you can determine what its height is. And you do this by what is given here as the height. Understand?"

"Yes," Sammy said, writing furiously, already thinking about the next day in school when he was going to volunteer to answer.

"Now," Manny continued, "you got the height, and the base is given, so you multiply the base times the height, and that gives you the area of the rectangle. Then to get the area of the triangle, which is inside the imaginary rectangle, you just multiply half the base times the height. That's it. Got it?"

"Yeah," Sammy said. Then he read and reread what he had written—Manny's words verbatim. He closed the book, satisfied he would impress his teacher.

With the lights out, Manny and Sammy lay in bed listening to the radio. Billy Eckstein sang softly in the background. Sammy, unable to sleep, examined a plate in the ceiling. The plate covered a hole where a light had been. Sammy always fixed on it when he went to bed. In the dark it had a different appearance. It looked like a face because of shadows and the bits of light that peeked through the room. It reminded him of the door at the synagogue.

"Manny, you up?"

"No. Manny's dead."

"I'm serious."

"I'm Roebuck. Who's minding the store?"

"Manny," Sammy implored.

"Okay, what is it?"

"Do you think those two people tonight are okay?"

"What people?"

"The colored man and his wife."

"Oh, yeah, they're okay."

"I think they were upset."

"Yeah, well, so was I."

"Yeah, but they were nice."

Manny got up, turned on the light, and turned down the radio.

"Well, little brother, so am I. But you don't see me knocking on other people's doors and telling them their religion isn't worth a shit, do you?"

Sammy hesitated.

"Well, do you?" Manny asked.

"No," Sammy said softly.

"Well, take this as a lesson then. If you want to dance, you gotta pay the band!"

"What does that mean?" Sammy asked.

Manny turned off the light and lay back down.

"It means that if you stick your neck out like that, you should be willing to take whatever someone has to give back. In this instance, it's me. Screw 'em."

"I was scared," Sammy said. Manny rose again and turned on the light.

"What for?" he asked more softly.

"I don't know. I just was."

Manny sat at the edge of his bed and looked at his younger brother in the bed across. Then he stood, walked over to Sammy, and sat beside him.

"Hey, it's nothing to worry about. I just did something, and it went too far. Nobody got hurt, except for some feelings—that's all. And I feel like shit about it. And Dad's a little pissed. But he's been pissed before, right?"

"Yeah, right," Sammy said with a laugh.

"Okay?"

"Okay," Sammy answered.

Manny turned out the light again. Sammy thought for a second and then said, "One more question."

"What?" Manny asked.

"What if you saw a picture of Eisenhower on a bathroom door? What would you do?"

"What?"

"If you saw a picture of Dwight Eisenhower on a bathroom door, what would you do?" Sammy asked.

"I'd finish crapping, wipe my ass, and flush the toilet," Manny answered.

"No, really, what would you do?"

"Nothing. I wouldn't give a shit."

"But if it wasn't supposed to be there?"

"Oh, that's a very different picture," Manny offered sarcastically. "I'd be very upset. I'd salute, probably try to call Mamie at the White House. 'Hey, Mamie, Dwight has his face on the shithouse door.'"

Sammy laughed. "Wouldn't you tell someone?"

"Yes," Manny said, ready to end the conversation so he could get some sleep. "I would tell the person in charge, the janitor, or someone who could make a decision about getting rid of it. It's disrespectful. Okay?"

"Okay," Sammy said softly.

"Now let me get some zzz's. Good night."

Sammy turned his head and looked out the window. He could hear the traffic dimly in the background echoing from Broadway.

4

Sammy always entered Miss Cannon's math class with a sense of foreboding. He never made eye contact. If she was by the door, he would lower his head and slide into his seat, open his book, and read over the material as if, by some miracle, one morning might be different, as if one morning he might actually have learned something about math. Math was difficult because it wasn't in English. Science was difficult, but at least he could read it, even memorize it. But math had to be figured out, and he simply couldn't do it. Whenever something new was introduced, the students invariably were asked if they had any questions, and Sammy desperately wanted to raise his hand. But the problem was he had too many questions, the first one being, "Could you start all over again from the beginning?" He never had the courage to ask that, and he didn't want to be humiliated.

Miss Cannon was tough. She kept her white hair pulled back, causing her eyes to narrow and reminding him of the front end of a 1947 Pontiac. She never smiled, except one time when Audrey Rabinowitz sang "When Irish Eyes Are Smiling" for her. So every day, Sammy prayed for the bell to end his misery, determined that when he did his homework that night, he would read the chapter until he understood, but he rarely got past the first page before numbers were introduced, and then all hope was lost.

This time, as he entered the class, he possessed even more than the usual fear. He had the answer to a homework problem, and he was going to volunteer to give it. It would be a first. As usual he went directly to his seat and aligned his head behind the student in front of him so as not to be noticed. While most of the students in the class reviewed their homework or exchanged opinions on the previous night's TV shows, Sammy focused on his math problem. He read over the solution to the area of a triangle line by line, just as Manny had taught him. He took a deep breath and realized just how nervous he was, so he took another deep breath, let it out slowly, and his nose twitched.

A feeling of gloom swept over him as the bell rang. Excited that he would impress his teacher for the first time, he also wished there was no such thing as a math class. Why couldn't he just play stickball? For an instant the prison cell came into his mind, where he could be rolling dice and playing his baseball game.

"Alright, class. CLASS!" Miss Cannon said, raising her voice.

She flipped through the textbook. "What was the assignment for last night?"

"One through six in chapter 7," someone volunteered.

"Oh, yes, thank you."

Sammy began reading the answer to himself again. He could hear the class going over the problems, but it was distant, almost like background music.

"Who would like to answer the first one?" Miss Cannon asked.

Hands rose. Sammy looked up, then looked back at his paper and studied again the answer to the question he would tackle. The next question passed, and the next, and his heart was near racing as Miss Cannon came to the fourth problem.

"Alright, number four. Anyone? The area of a triangle. A bit tricky. Who would like to handle this one?"

Sammy's heart was pounding. He reached for the ceiling, peering at Miss Cannon intently so that she would be persuaded to call on him. Their eyes met, but she passed over him, and then in a double-take, she looked at him again and stopped. Surprise came over her, and then a hint of a smile. It was perhaps one of those moments in a teacher's career when she discovers a change, a revelation, a leap in one of her students that goes down as a story told to future classes. So she pointed to him. "Yes, Mr. Levitt?" she asked, still a bit unsure. "Would you like to answer number four?"

"Yes," he said, rising slowly and turning his paper so that he could read it. All eyes turned toward him. He met some of them and felt embarrassed by the attention, but pleased that it wasn't for being unable to answer a question. A few students could be heard chatting.

"Shhh!" Miss Cannon demanded.

He began. "To get the area of a triangle, you must first draw imaginary lines to make a rectangle around the triangle." He hesitated a bit for effect. "This is accomplished by extending a line from the base of the triangle to the height of the top of the triangle on both sides. Since the height is ten inches and the base is twenty inches, you..." He paused again for effect, trying not to appear too sure. "You multiply them to get the area of a rectangle." He paused again. His heart slowed. He felt rather comfortable now.

"Now to get the area of a triangle, you divide the area of the rectangle by two, which equals 100 inches." He looked at Miss Cannon and then down at his paper. He could hear the class whispering, and he was sure it was about him. A feeling of satisfaction came over him. Perhaps he sounded like Rod or Abby Finkle, who were the ones who usually whipped off answers to math questions.

Miss Cannon rose from her seat and walked to the front of her desk. She lifted her heavy frame onto the edge of the oak and looked at the class, her hands folded on her lap. Then she looked at Sammy.

"Well, that was outstanding, Mr. Levitt," she said. "You seem to have done your homework. That was a difficult problem, and you seem to have handled it well. I'm impressed." She paused for a moment, then walked back to her seat and looked at the text. "Let's see," she said idly.

"Class, does anyone have any questions on how to find the area of a rectangle? Now that was a simpler problem, one we just tackled a minute ago before Mr. Levitt tackled the more difficult problem of finding the area of a triangle." Sammy felt good all over as he sat in his chair and met his teacher's eyes directly, feeling for once a part of the class. A few hands rose and Miss Cannon called on one. The student asked if Miss Cannon could go over the area of a rectangle one more time.

"I don't see why not. Mr. Levitt," she said, looking at Sammy, "since you worked the area of a triangle so beautifully, would you be kind enough to show the class how to find the area of a rectangle? That's number two in your text, I believe."

Sammy stared at Miss Cannon in disbelief. The blood drained from his face. Outside a plane flew overhead; Sammy imagined himself inside it. He thought of the pilot, the controls, and then he thought of the prison cell. A ringing in his ear temporarily blocked out all sound from the class. He felt flush, hot in his cheeks and head. He rose, staring at the back of the girl who sat in front of him. He looked at her sweater, staring at the floral design, and counted three roses—three of them. Then he looked at the question in his textbook. It was similar to the one he'd answered. Maybe he could figure it out. He stared at his explanation for the area of a triangle, but didn't know where to begin. As he stared at the page he could see the floral design of the sweater and counted the roses again and again. He just stood there silently.

"So, Mr. Levitt?"

He said nothing, just looked up and stared at Miss Cannon.

"It's easier to find the area of a rectangle than a triangle, Mr. Levitt. How can you answer one question and not the other?"

The class began to whisper again. He knew it wasn't admiration this time. How could I do this?, he thought. He played back the night before, imagined Manny teaching him this problem as well so he would be prepared. He wished he'd asked Manny to explain it until he understood.

"So?" the teacher asked, this time much louder.

"I can't," he said in a low voice.

"What?"

"I can't," he said, clearing his throat.

"That's ridiculous. You just described the area of a triangle!" she shouted. He wanted her to stop.

"The area of a rectangle is the multiplication of the sides. How can you not know that and find the area of a triangle? How? Tell me!"

He looked at the page and blinked his eyes, trying to hold back the tears.

Miss Cannon was furious as she looked around the room and pointed to another student.

"Joyce, please answer the question for the class." Miss Cannon didn't look at him as he sank into his chair, hoping everyone would forget this moment.

He realized that he was breathing hard, but he was grateful that it was over. For now, he could relax. He would not be called on again. He knew that. In fact, Miss Cannon refused to look at him for the rest of the hour. He just sat there looking at the girl's hair in front of him, noticing for the first time the different shades of light brown and blonde as they lay evenly on her shoulders. And as he sat there, he wondered if Miss Cannon hated him, and whether, if he saw her in the street after school, should he say hello? Would she want him to or would she be disgusted? They only like smart kids, he thought. He would cross the street.

5

The schoolyard was near empty when Sammy arrived Saturday morning, just a few younger kids playing basketball. He sat down and leaned against the fence, bouncing a Spaldeen in front of him and still hoping there was a stickball game left in the season. He looked at his watch. Nine o'clock. It was early. As if startled, he jumped up and left the schoolyard and headed south toward the shule. He walked past the Christian Science church, past the newsstand, and stopped in front of the shule. He looked down the hill towards St. Mary's, the local Catholic church. Then he turned and entered the synagogue. Al, the janitor, was on his way out of the building. He wore a yarmulke. Sammy had for a long time wondered whether he was Jewish. Sammy had heard there were black Jews in Harlem. He wanted to ask Al about the door, but was afraid. Al never smiled, never talked to the kids, only yelled at them. He always seemed to be angry. Sammy wanted to say hello to him at times but always held back.

Sammy sat down in front of the rabbi's door and looked at it, turning his head. It still looked like Jesus, he thought. He could see a beard, and he wondered if all the pictures he had seen of Jesus had a beard. Why didn't they have pictures of him as an old man? The door to the sanctuary opened, and the cantor's voice poured out. Sammy continued to examine the image ingrained into the wood on the rabbi's door. A large knot served as the right eye, a smaller one served as the left, so that the face appeared more like a profile. The beard appeared where the grain narrowed and faded at the bottom of Jesus' chin. Sammy wondered why he had been the only one to notice. Or maybe he hadn't. Maybe the rabbi had seen it himself. Or Al. Or the painter.

Sammy stepped outside again, looked toward the schoolyard, checked his watch, and then looked south. The Catholic church was built of dark brown stone, a kind seen only in older construction. It was a single-story structure, about the size of a very large house, built to serve a small community at the turn of the century, probably before a Jew even saw the neighborhood. It was guarded by a small, manicured lawn surrounded by a tall, black, wrought-iron fence. The way the neighborhood had grown up around it with newsstands, grocery stores, and subway stations, it looked like a water lily resting in a cesspool.

Sammy had always been taken by the sign outside the church that forecast the topic of the sermon approaching, especially when the sermon offered proof of the existence of God. He couldn't remember seeing a synagogue with such a sign. The idea of going inside to find the answers to the questions posed on the sign intrigued him. Occasionally, on a Sunday, he would pass by and see a few parishioners exiting the church, but he didn't know the kids. There was a rumor that they were going to close it because of low attendance, but those rumors had been rife since he came to the neighborhood. Since the war, so many German Jews moved to the area that it was often referred to as the "Fourth Reich."

He walked through the gate and headed for the large wooden door. He stopped and gazed at the designs and the metal attachments that adorned it. It smelled of age and history and made him think of the new, cold, blue metal doors of the shule, each with a small square window, the glass lined with thin wires for strength. Sammy looked around and placed his Spaldeen neatly behind a bush so that it wouldn't roll. He lifted the large metal knocker and let it smack the door. He rocked from side to side and wrinkled his nose, waiting for someone to come. But no one did, so he pushed the door open.

He was surprised at the size of the place—so small, he thought—and the odor of the incense. He had never smelled anything like it. But he liked it. As he inched in, slowly passing the burning candles, he thought of the old shule—not the odor, but the old wood and the carpeting, much nicer. This was no basement. He walked cautiously on the worn carpet. Paintings of biblical scenes he had not seen before covered the walls. The pictures appeared to be very old with thick gilt frames that spoke of authenticity.

Walking down the right side of the sanctuary toward the altar, he tripped over a hole in the carpet, stamping his foot into the floor. He looked to see if anyone had heard. A woman stood up, crossed herself, and turned to walk out. As she passed him, she smiled. He stood with his mouth open. Where did she come from? he wondered. Did she know he was Jewish? He gathered his wits and walked further, through a closed door, down a hall, and past another door. At the sound of a typewriter, he relaxed a bit, thinking he wasn't trespassing.

He knocked on the door and heard the typewriter stop. His heart began to race. The door opened and a gray-haired lady appeared before him.

"Can I help you?" she asked.

Sammy looked at her and realized he was not prepared. "The priest—" he stumbled. "Please." The lady placed her hand on his shoulder, leaned over him, and pointed down the hall.

"Watch out for those pails," she said, pointing to two buckets, an inch of water in each, brown stains in the ceiling above.

Sammy maneuvered around the pails and came to another door.

He heard a radio playing. He worried about whether he was allowed to be there and about what the priest would do if he found out he was Jewish. Or if Rabbi Gold found out he was here. What would the rabbi do? Then Sammy thought of his friends and Lyn Rosen, who he wanted for a girlfriend but had never had the courage to ask. But then, he'd never had a date and wasn't old enough.

While he stood there contemplating, the noise of the radio sank in. It was a familiar sound—sports. Then it stopped, and a man's voice could be heard. It was too early for a game. Then he heard another man's voice.

"Bullshit. Kiss my fat Irish ass." It clearly was not on the radio.

Sammy became tense. The priest was angry. Then came a loud, "Jesus Christ!"

Maybe this wasn't a good time.

He was still standing frozen before the door when it opened. A large man with a reddish complexion and thinning, blondish-white hair burst out, almost knocking Sammy over. A broad smile broke across his face when he saw the shocked child before him. It was a handsome face, hardened by lines, but with bright white teeth that Sammy could admire, because they didn't have any gaps like his own.

"Here to confess, my boy?"

Amazing, Sammy thought. How could he know?

"Yes," Sammy answered rather shyly.

The priest placed his arm around Sammy's shoulder and walked him back toward the chapel. Sammy looked at the man's robe. It reminded him of the rabbi's suit. It had the same shine. The sleeves were fraying a bit as well.

"Where are we going?" Sammy asked.

"Confession," the priest answered, rather surprised.

They walked a few more steps.

"Can't we just talk about it right here?"

The priest laughed and coaxed him forward. Sammy moved along. After a step or two the priest stopped.

"Who are your parents, son?"

"Sid and Mara Levitt."

"'Levitt'...huh...mmm... I gather that they are not parishioners here," he said with a hint of a smile.

"Oh, no, we go to the Fort Washington Jewish Center."

"And your name?"

Sammy told him.

"Well, then, why do you want to confess, Sammy? Shouldn't you be talking with Rabbi Gold? He's your rabbi, isn't he?"

"Yeah, but I don't think that's a good idea."

"And why is that?"

"I think it concerns you more than it concerns him, and besides, I don't think he'll be so happy about it." More relaxed now, Sammy moved down a bit as he talked and wandered over to the confessional. "What's that?" he asked.

"Confessional. That was where I was taking you. "

"Well, I think we should talk there then. This is private and very important."

The priest agreed, pointing the way. The priest looked up at the ceiling, examined the confessional, turned, and smiled. "Let's use this one. You go in there." The priest entered the other side, removed a handkerchief, and stuck it into the broken partition.

Sammy sat down, looked around, and touched the wood. Graffiti was covering the once highly polished wood, giving it the worn appearance of a school desk. "Remember Grant, Remember Lee. If you need money, Remember Grant." "Father

Casey sucks." Sammy started to chuckle and then remembered the priest. Sammy pulled at the handkerchief and felt it pull back, so he pulled it again.

"What are you doing?" the priest asked.

"Oh, I'm sorry. I can't see you."

"That's the way it's supposed to be, son."

"Sorry."

"That's okay." The priest thought for a moment and then began.

"Yes, my son, what is it you want to confess?"

"Well, sir, it's not really a confession. I saw something, and I thought you ought to know about it." He stopped and thought for a second about what he had just said. Why would the priest want to know? Why should he know? Then Sammy wished that he had asked his father. He would have known what to do. Suddenly Sammy felt frightened but he didn't know why.

"Well, tell me. What did you see?" the priest asked gently.

Sammy sat frozen, thinking about the door.

"Sammy?"

"Uhhh..." Sammy wondered what would happen if he bolted from the booth. Could the priest catch him? Probably not. But the priest already knew his parents' names. He'd call the rabbi, and then he would be in real trouble. Sammy sagged a bit, then spoke.

"Well, your honor, they're finishing the new synagogue at 184th—you know, by the subway stop?"

The priest looked at his watch.

"Yes, yes, go on."

"Well, there's a lot of building and banging, and there's this door—the rabbi's door—that has a picture on it."

"Yes, yes," the priest said, shifting in his seat. "Go on, please."

"Well, this door..."

"Yes?" Much louder now.

"Well, this door has a picture of Jesus on it."

The priest said nothing. And then after a few moments he asked, "What is a picture of Jesus doing in a rabbi's office?"

"It's not in his office. It's on his office door."

"What's the difference? 'In' the office, 'on' the office... What's it doing there? That doesn't make any sense."

Sammy shrugged his shoulders, as if the priest could see him to read his expression.

"Well, this makes no sense. Why are you telling me this? Why don't you tell your rabbi? This is ridiculous. Do your parents know that you're here?" he asked, obviously irritated.

"No, sir."

"Well, why does the rabbi have a picture of Jesus on his door?"

"I don't know if he knows it."

"That makes no sense either. How could he not know it? Is he blind?"

Sammy sat motionless, wondering why the priest was so angry. This was not what he had envisioned, and he was afraid.

"Well?" the priest urged.

Sammy rose slowly. "I gotta go," he mumbled.

"I think that's best," the priest replied.

As Sammy inched out of the confessional, the priest called after him, "This makes no sense at all. Why would a picture of Jesus be tacked on a door in a synagogue?" First the radio had pissed him off and now Sammy.

"It's not tacked," Sammy answered.

"What was that?"

"I said it's not tacked."

"What's not tacked?"

"The picture." Sammy turned to leave.

The priest exited the booth, a quizzical look on his face. "Wait a minute," he said.

Sammy stopped.

"What do you mean 'it's not tacked'?" the priest asked.

"Just what I said. It's not tacked. It's in the door."

The priest walked carefully toward Sammy, then put a hand on each of Sammy's shoulders.

"You mean to tell me that this picture is 'in' the door? Exactly how is it 'in' the door? Please explain it to me," he urged gently.

"It's not a poster, sir. It's in the door."

The priest leaned back against the confessional, sat down, and motioned Sammy to do the same. Sammy sat down on his side of the booth so they were back where they started.

"What do you mean 'in the door'?" the priest asked.

"It's a picture in the grain of the door." The priest leaned back in his seat and crossed himself.

"You mean there's no poster?"

"No."

"No painting?" the priest asked even more gently.

"No."

Sammy sat expectantly and pulled on the handkerchief to see if something was wrong. The priest ran his fingers nervously through his thinning hair, saw the handkerchief move, and pulled it back.

"No!" the priest said sharply, scaring Sammy. "I'm sorry," he said. "You aren't supposed to see me."

"Oh," Sammy said, and folded his hands. "Is it okay? I mean, I just saw you outside."

"Yes, yes, I'm just thinking. Just a minute, son. This is very important. Thank you."

Sammy sat back and stared at the graffiti. "If you want a blow job, call..." He covered his mouth and laughed.

"You say it's a door?"

"Yes, sir."

"The rabbi's door?" the priest asked. "How many people know this?"

"I don't know. Maybe only me." Sammy thought for a moment. "Yeah, probably only me, 'cause you gotta look at it on kind of an angle."

"Angle? Oh, yes, I see," the priest said. He looked at the ceiling and fixed on the peeling paint, and stains from leaks that had been fixed, and new ones just beginning.

"Sammy," the priest continued cautiously, "are you sure it wasn't the Virgin Mary?"

Sammy had read all the graffiti. He took a deep breath, almost from boredom now as he had to repeat it. "Yes. It's in the grain, you know. Maybe it's nothing. I gotta go now." He bent down to pick up his ball and remembered that he had left it outside.

"No, no, wait, Sammy. I meant are you sure it wasn't a woman?"

"If it's a woman, she's got a great beard. Can I go now?" Sammy imagined himself tossing his Spaldeen before him as he walked up Fort Washington Avenue. He felt like bolting.

"Well, son, sometimes people see visions of Mary with a little baby. It's quite common, you know."

Sammy nodded, again as if the priest could see him.

"Sammy, I want you to keep this our little secret, okay?" the priest continued.

"Okay," Sammy said, and with that he got up from his seat.

"Is that a deal, son?"

Sammy yanked the handkerchief from the hole between them and stuck his arm through to shake the priest's hand. "Deal," Sammy said. After a few seconds a hand met his and shook it. Sammy pulled his arm back and walked out of the confessional. The priest met him in the aisle. "You need to fix that hole," Sammy said.

The priest smiled and looked at the ceiling thoughtfully. "We will, Sammy," he said. "We will." He stood with arms crossed as he watched Sammy exit. "Remember, Sammy," he said as Sammy pushed at the door, "please don't tell anyone. I will take care of it. You did the right thing coming to me."

"Okay," Sammy said, looking back one last time and thinking he would never see the priest again.

Sammy left the church quickly and, just as quickly, the whole idea left his mind. Now he could think about more important things, like the Dodgers, homework, and Lyn.

6

Sammy saw the small pink envelope on his bed and knew instantly what it was. There had lately been a bounty of parties given by the most popular girls in the seventh-grade class. Being invited rekindled the feeling he'd had when he first arrived in the neighborhood and could punch a ball to the outfield. For a short time he was popular. He was popular mainly because of sports. And though he was short, Sammy was considered cute, and there were two girls in the class he could fit with according to height.

At square dancing and other co-ed school activities, he was generally paired with one of those two girls. Sammy was the second shortest boy in class, a status he contemplated carefully during fire drills and anything else that required lining up. He looked at the student next to him, who was clearly and inch or two shorter, and he would nearly sigh from relief that it wasn't him in that spot. Being the shortest seemed to him somehow ugly. And yet as he watched Shelley, his closest friend, begin to grow taller, Sammy found himself having less in common with him, so that their housing proximity was becoming the only hold on their sliding friendship.

But the invitation was from Lyn Rosen, the girl he dreamed about. Lyn was not short. She was inches taller than he, slim with a short haircut and bangs that fell over her eyes. She was shy and looked away and down when she smiled. And she smiled at him, and he smiled back, and at that time, and at that age, it was the closest thing to "going together," though they hardly exchanged a word.

At night, as Sammy lay in bed looking at the ceiling, he would think of Lyn and imagine himself naked with her. Sometimes he couldn't wait to get to bed, for it was the closest he could get to a sexual experience.

It was eight o'clock when he approached the entrance to Lyn's white brick building on Cabrini Boulevard. Inside at the mirror separating the two elevator doors leading up to her apartment, he examined his reflection and adjusted his tie. As he did so, his nose twitched, exposing the gap between his teeth, and he decided he'd smile with his mouth shut if he could. But he liked his curved pompadour, and how shiny his hair was from the Vitalis.

Upstairs as he left the elevator, he looked left, then right, for her apartment. He rang the doorbell, hoping he wasn't early. When the door opened, he found himself staring at Lyn. She smiled and bowed her head.

"Hi," he said.

Lyn welcomed him in. As he passed her, he saw her mother in the kitchen, smiling. He walked into the living room, past a bowl of potato chips and a bowl of punch. He was the first boy to arrive. All the girls who were invited were already there, standing in the corner, laughing and whispering. They appeared overdressed. Most were wearing pinafores, which reminded him of beach umbrellas and made them appear like little girls. And all seemed to have a ribbon somewhere. He stood awkwardly for a bit, then sat down behind the chips. Lyn came over to him and offered him some popcorn.

"No, thanks, I don't like popcorn," he said, and then wished he hadn't. Lyn took the bowl away and joined the girls in the corner. Sammy stood and went to the mantle. He tried to lean his elbow on it, but it was too tall, so he placed his hands behind him and looked at the painting on the wall above the couch. He tried to think about what he should do or say. He couldn't remember talking to any of these girls in class except to borrow something. His relationship with girls had been limited to looking athletic during dodgeball, which was one of the few co-ed activities.

Lyn's mother peeked around the corner to examine the level of punch and chips. She placed a small bowl of Tootsie Rolls on the table and saw Sammy looking at her in the large mirror in the foyer. She smiled at him, and he returned the smile but was embarrassed, being seen standing alone instead of engaging in conversation. The doorbell rang, and Sammy peered eagerly toward the entrance. Lyn opened the door and let Marc Jacoby inside. Suddenly Marc, a kid he hardly knew, was destined to be his closest friend for a few moments. He was a boy, and they could talk. Sammy watched as Lyn marched Marc through the same ritual.

Soon the room was filled with kids, and Sammy's comfort had risen with each new boy who entered the apartment. Ten boys on one side of the room talking about sports, and ten girls on the other side talking about boys.

Lyn's mother appeared again at the entrance of the foyer and drew a disapproving glance from Lyn. Sammy watched as her mother slinked out of the room, presumably for good. Then Lyn called for attention and had everyone draw lots for which circle to sit in while they played spin-the-bottle, saving herself for last and not drawing a lot, but merely slipping into Sammy's circle and sitting opposite him. Sammy looked at her and smiled, then looked away, but he couldn't keep his eyes off her. Back and forth he would look and then get caught looking and look away.

Someone picked up the empty Pepsi bottle and spun it. Sammy watched as it twirled around, hoping it would point to him. The bottle stopped in front of one girl more than most and everyone laughed. Finally the bottle pointed to Sammy. He felt a twitch coming on, so he lowered his head. Then he graciously accepted a kiss from Carol. Eventually the bottle landed on Sammy and Lyn, but they never got the spin he wanted. Later, Lyn's mother called for a break, and they each looked at each other and shrugged their shoulders. Maybe they'd play post office, he thought.

Sammy picked up a glass of punch and wandered over to a bunch of guys admiring the breasts of Roseanne Diamond. She was the first girl to blossom that way, and she seemed to have become the most popular girl in the class. He could hardly remember her from the year before.

The party resumed by breaking up into two groups again, this time to play post office. Lyn placed herself in the other group, and Sammy wondered why. She sat with her back to him. He could see her silky, short black hair move from side to side as she spirited her circle along. Sammy began to make jokes, determined to have a good time without her. Besides, he could stare at her more easily now, since she could no longer see him. Maybe she sat in that circle because she had to, he thought. Maybe it was nothing. And for a few moments he felt relaxed and actually enjoyed himself, at least until he saw someone get up to kiss her because he was the postman. Had she sat there because she was hoping he would kiss her, Sammy wondered, or was it the luck of the draw?

"Sammy, it's your turn."

"Oh," he said as he came back to reality.

By ten o'clock, the party had found its rhythm, but Lyn's mother came out and, glancing at Lyn, pointed to the silver watch on her wrist. Lyn excused herself and entered the kitchen, where Sammy heard a small battle ensue. Moments later Lyn returned, this time apologizing for ending the party. Everybody stood up and talked about the party being fun, as Lyn's mother brought out the coats and jackets. Sammy stood around engaging some in conversation, anxiously avoiding his coat in hopes of being the last to leave.

Shelley put on his coat, shook Lyn's hand at the door, and looked at Sammy. He looked around and saw two girls from the building helping Lyn's mother clean up and realized that they would be here for a while, probably to talk with Lyn about the party, so he nodded to Shelley and walked to the door.

"Thank you for inviting me," Sammy said, looking at her bangs as her head leaned downward. He could see her smile. His nose twitched, but to his relief, the angle of her head prevented her from seeing above his neck. He wanted to kiss her, but he thought of Shelley standing there. Instead he held her hand. Would Shelley feel uncomfortable if he kissed her? He wondered. Sammy was still holding her hand when he turned and said goodbye. Shelley was holding the elevator door for him. As Sammy walked toward it, he saw what he thought was a look of disappointment on Lyn's face. He wanted to turn around, walk back, and kiss her. Shelley began talking about something that happened at the party, but Sammy wasn't listening. His thoughts were fixed on Lyn. I should turn around, he thought. He looked at Shelley, turned, but saw that Lyn was already closing the door. Wait, he thought, but said nothing. He stood frozen, and he heard Shelley call again. He entered the elevator angry at not kissing Lyn, and angry at Shelley, then angry at himself for worrying about Shelley.

Later that evening, as he rested his head under his hands and gazed up at the shadows on the ceiling with the lights out, he thought of Lyn. He pictured himself talking to her in school the next day. He saw himself explaining to her why he didn't kiss her, and in his mind she responded well. In fact, she'd tell him how much she wanted to kiss him. As they talked, they inched around a corner of the hallway and kissed. Only it was more than a kiss, and as they laid their books down, they slinked to the floor in an embrace, the taste of each other's lips on their tongues melding for many slow, agonizing minutes—and it was wonderful. He touched his crotch, stiff now with excitement, and began the scenario over again, this time fast-forwarding to the kissing part, happy as he drifted off to sleep.

7

Stan Leopold turned from the phone flashing for his attention and looked over Central Park. He focused on the treetops so that he could imagine nothing else. And as the city of New York disappeared from his view, he felt the calm that he counted on when he looked out this window. Forty stories high was his minimum—what he insisted on when he was offered the job of director of one of the most prestigious Jewish organizations. In its hunger for a new, post-war look, the organization gave Leopold what he wanted. The American Jewish Association would be a modern organization with closer contacts to power.

Stan looked down to his shoes and checked his shine. He still bought his clothes from the little shops he had frequented since his days in high school.

"Dreck," his father said. "What's wrong with Crawford's or Bond's?" But the big men's stores didn't carry what he wanted. He didn't wear Florsheim shoes, but instead went to a store on 46th Street where he could find what was advertised in *Esquire*. His ties, the umbrella with the bone handle that stood in the brass bowl in the corner, his pants, his shirt—they all came from places he sought out. He looked at clothes the way some men look at cars. They were not just a means of transportation, but an element of his identity. He didn't tell anyone where he bought his clothes.

He bought his first pair of pants on 14th Street when he was seventeen. He was in his last year of high school, and he and his father walked into a small shop with clothes piled in uneven stacks leaning against each other for support. Stan picked out the pair he wanted, a brown pair of gabardines. His father examined the pants, first the cut, then the material, and then told Stan to put them on. He looked at Stan, touching the pants to see if they fit correctly. Stan stood silently, wishing his father wouldn't be so thorough. Then his father looked at the salesman and asked, "Nu, how much?"

The salesman realized he was in the company of a tradesman, probably not a manufacturer of clothing, judging from his clothes and the way he looked. He didn't have the polish that an uptown manufacturer might normally display, but he could have been someone who worked for a manufacturer. He knew value just the same.

"Eighteen dollars," the salesman said. A large sum for a pair of pants. Stan remembered feeling embarrassed and wanting to disappear into the pants, for he knew what his father's reaction would be.

"Eighteen dollars? I don't want to be a partner!" Stan's father said. The salesman smiled, relaxing for the first time.

"We sell to young people," and with that he shrugged, as if to apologize.

"Wonderful," Stan's father said in his thick Polish accent. "I'm not so young. Vie fiel? You can do better."

The salesman looked at the code on the label written in pencil, shook his head, and said, "Ten dollars, but I can't do any better than that, and I can't alter."

"I believe you," his father answered sarcastically, feeling Stan's leg again and turning him around. Stan vowed then and there never to shop with his father again.

"So, you like them?" Stan's father asked.

"Yes."

"Alright," his father said and gave the man ten dollars, which the man put in his pocket.

Stan sighed with relief, the dealing complete.

His father said, "Nice pants. Enjoy it in good health." Then he placed his hand on his son's neck, giving it an affectionate squeeze, and they walked out of the store. Stan was embarrassed by his father. He wasn't like the dads he saw in the movies. He was opinionated and always had an answer, whether right or wrong. But that's the way it was, he thought. We didn't act like the others.

Stan picked up the *Daily News* that was lying on his desk and read the bold headline again. It was already three days old: "Jewish Boy Sees Vision of Jesus." He shook his head and dropped the paper. It was time to leave the office. He adjusted his tie.

"I'm going to lunch, Linda, and then to the meeting."

"What about all the calls? What should I tell them?"

"Tell them I'm dead."

Linda stopped what she was doing and laughed.

"Tell them I'm on it. Tell them anything," he said in a more serious tone.

Stan walked into the bar at the Carlyle Hotel. He blinked his eyes as they adjusted to the darkness, then took a seat in the corner surrounded by the Ludwig Bemelmans murals and ordered a ginger ale. Life could be better, he thought, but he sure couldn't figure out how, except for ignoring this recent unpleasantness. He swirled his drink and waited. He was as surprised as anyone of the events in his life and how one thing had led to another, most of it unplanned, and how he had jumped at opportunities that brought him to where he was. People admired how he had become so successful so fast, but he'd simply taken a job here and there, and each job had led to something else. When people thought he was brilliant for making a certain move, he smiled. He'd simply been lucky, at the right place at the right time. It had been easy until now. He'd heard that some people were wondering if this would all blow up in his face.

Stan heard the door open and saw John Sticker come through and look around. He lifted his glass so that John could find him.

"How the hell are you?" Sticker asked, shaking Stan's hand and grabbing his arm affectionately.

"What'dya know? What'dya say?" he continued.

"Not much. I was just sitting here thinking about my father and realized that he probably never had a drink outside of his home."

"Geography was not a problem for my dad," Sticker said as he ran his finger inside his clerical collar and laughed.

"What was your father?"

"You mean, what *is* my father."

"He's still alive?" Stan asked, amazed.

Sticker looked around for a waiter.

"Do I look that decrepit?"

Stan laughed. "No, not really, but he must be pretty old."

"Well, actually he's ninety-four. He was a conductor on the first subway in New York. I think that was 1904. Just got off the boat and landed a job because of a cousin, who knew a cousin, who knew a cousin, who knew the sister of some big shot. Irishman, of course."

"Of course."

"So where is he?"

"He lives with my younger brother."

"I was just thinking of my dad and how embarrassed I always was when we were out in public. When I look back, I realize I was embarrassed because he had a personality. All I wanted was to become invisible."

"Embarrassment doesn't come to mind with my dad. I believe the word we're looking for here is 'fear.'"

"It's funny. I know where stereotypes come from: reality."

"Can I write that down?" Sticker asked, amused.

"Well, it's funny, that's all. I don't know. I talk this way whenever my world comes crashing down on me. Anyway, what's happening with you?"

"Same old. What about you?" he asked, with a sarcastic smile.

"Oh, not much. Only Jesus is back, and this time he may be playing stickball in Washington Heights."

Sticker laughed and turned around, looking for the waiter. The waiter saw him and headed for the bar without even asking what he wanted.

A few minutes later he returned with a glass of scotch on the rocks and placed it in front of the priest.

John stared at the scotch. "You see that?" he asked, pointing to the glass. "Two men sitting and drinking. One, a real man, is drinking a glass of scotch, single malt, I believe. At least twelve years old. The other is drinking a glass of...what is that, a urine sample?"

"In my defense," Stan answered, "my father drank exactly like you do—a glass of schnapps that would straighten the hairs on that pecker of yours that still wears a cap, I believe. Now I admit, coming from a more reasonable group of people, he usually had his hand on a glass instead of a bottle, and I might add, always in a prone position."

The priest lifted his glass as in a toast, and he said laughing, "You know, Stan, there's a reason I keep you around. You make me laugh."

Sticker became serious. He stirred his drink, then looked at Stan.

"So how are you, really? What's been going on at your end?" he asked. "How serious is this?"

Stan shrugged. "It's such a pain in the ass. I mean, what do you do? Nothing like this has ever happened before. How do you deal with it? I'm sure your people aren't happy about this."

"Some are," Sticker said with a smile. "Some are very happy. You're always gonna have some who eat this stuff up."

"So far there's just confusion, but I imagine all hell is going to break loose. I'm told that already there's been a gathering of people this morning and yesterday who are just gawking at the synagogue, trying to get in. This could get pretty ugly. What do you know?"

"Which part?"

"Well, can you tell me about the priest who called the press conference? Did you guys know he was gonna do that? What's his story?"

Sticker took a sip of his drink and ran his finger around his collar again. He took out a cigarette, tapped it on the table, and checked his pockets for a match.

"Here," Stan said, pulling a Ronson from his jacket.

"Thanks." Sticker took a puff and blew smoke to the ceiling. He offered Stan a cigarette, but he said he would smoke one later.

"So tell me," Stan urged.

"Well, as far as I know—and I can't swear by any of it, but it seems close to the truth—this is what happened: The kid thought it appropriate to tell a priest what he saw, and St. Mary's was the closest church to the scene. Believe me, Stan, I wish it were me he came to. And in answer to your question, no, we didn't know he was going to call a news conference. This guy was strictly on his own. This is not a church thing. He's a bit of a loose cannon."

"Who the hell is he?"

"Well, I actually know him...Father James Conway. A nice guy as I remember, and once a bright star, but there have been rumors that he got too close to a nun, and his career went on hold. He travels with her and it's possible they live together." He drew closer to Stan. "The guy is apparently practically married and can't give it up."

"That doesn't seem like a guy who would want to be noticed."

"Well, I think he's pissed off. The church would like to do something else with his building. The neighborhood has changed. Mostly Jewish, if you get my drift. No one goes there anymore. But as you well know, Rome moves slowly. In the meantime, they haven't made a repair to the building in years. I don't know anything else, except that he might have blown this thing out of proportion."

"Out of proportion? Jesus Christ, John, what I've been told was, he said something like there's a vision of Jesus. It wasn't a vision, John. The kid just said it looked like something."

"Hey, I didn't do anything. I only work here," Sticker said, raising his hands in surrender.

"It's too early, and probably nothing will happen, except I know that the priest is being quizzed as we speak."

Stan shook his head. "I don't know. I gotta talk to a whole bunch of people in one hour and give them something, and I don't know what to say. If war broke out in the Middle East I'd know just what to do. But this?"

"This is a ball buster, I grant you that. Just tell them you met with me, and things are being discussed. I'm a bishop, and that will tell them something."

"Yeah, but do they know you drink so much?"

"Don't your people think we all drink too much?" Sticker added, laughing.

"Shit, John, this could get nuts if I don't do something. We don't need a Lourdes on Fort Washington Avenue."

"Yeah, but think of all the revenue."

"Oh, shit," Stan said, exasperated.

Sticker caught the waiter's eye and asked for another. "You want another?" he asked Stan.

"Yeah, I'll have a ginger ale."

"How embarrassing."

Stan chuckled, his mood shifting from tension to relief.

"Listen, Stan. We don't want this any more than you do. Do you think the pope is gonna enjoy this? It's all a pain in the ass, but I don't know exactly how to resolve it. Listen, if Conway doesn't let up—I mean, if he doesn't give a shit—then it will be hard to stop him. Hell, it doesn't even meet the criteria for a vision."

"Criteria?"

"Yeah," Sticker said more seriously. "There are rules for these occurrences. Never mind. That's not your headache. We'll see how it develops, and I will try to help things along."

"Are you gonna eat or just sit here and bust my balls?"

"I'd better."

"Better what? Eat or bust my balls?"

"Well, now that you mention it, busting your balls holds an attraction, but I gotta eat something." The waiter placed a new glass before Sticker and asked if he needed anything else.

"Yeah, George, I think we're gonna eat something. Stan, see anything?" Stan laid down the menu and said, "Bring me the vichyssoise if you don't mind. That's cold, isn't it?" he asked, looking at the waiter.

"Yes, sir. And you, sir?"

"George, I think I'll have the same thing. That sounds good."

"Very well."

"My stomach is too jittery for anything else," Stan offered.

"Stan, relax. I'll really look into this. The Church appreciates visions but doesn't want a circus, and it looks a whole lot more authentic when the sightings are from peasants in France rather than Jewish boys from Manhattan, though I have to admit it's pretty damned cool."

"Oh, great!"

"Don't worry. Here!" he said, raising his glass for a toast. "To the next vision, and may it please be Mary!"

8

Stan could hear it from the elevator. He could differentiate between the normal buzz of a large group of men talking about various subjects and the sound of the same group arguing about a hot issue. This was more than a buzz. It was louder, with sharp rises like fireworks periodically rising in different locales. He could not remember it this loud before.

He patted down his hair, pulled a felt yarmulke from his jacket pocket, and placed it on the crown of his head. Then he smiled and opened the door. It was like entering into a sports arena. Suddenly he found himself enveloped in sound and people, as he was charged by those who saw him.

"So, what's this?" a man asked, showing him a headline.

"Don't worry, Sam."

"Don't worry, he says," the man said, speaking to no one in particular.

The room could hold about thirty comfortably, fifty in a pinch. Chairs lined the walls for older guests. As Stan headed for the podium, the doors in the rear swung open, and a long table covered with a white tablecloth was wheeled in. On it rested an array of bagels, lox, cream cheese, kippers, whitefish spread, and pastries, as well as a silver urn of coffee. The sound shifted a bit as attention shifted to the food. Stan saw an opportunity to change his direction and work the crowd.

"I have some information," he told someone pulling at his sleeve. "I'll tell you."

"It's not as bad as it seems," he told another, and to another he winked, as if to assure him that everything was under control.

It was at times like this when he had to be up to the task. He wasn't religious, and he was more aware of the Yiddish he couldn't speak than what little Yiddish he could. When he stood before Orthodox groups and Yiddish was spoken, he felt like an outsider as he steadfastly stood by.

When the food would no longer placate the audience, Stan edged towards the podium and grabbed the microphone. A loud screeching sound silenced the room immediately.

He thought for a second and then said, "Ma nish ta nor ha lila ha Ze? 'Why is this day different from all others?'" The room burst out in laughter, mostly from relief.

"In all candor, gentlemen, this is not a happy moment in our local history, and I surely do hope that this does not become even a footnote in Jewish history. For those of you who by some miracle have not heard the news, we are here today to discuss the events of this week—that is, the bar mitzvah boy in Washington Heights who saw a picture of Jesus." Immediately the crowd began to yell and argue with each other, and Stan raised his arms for quiet. Then he tapped the mike.

"Alright...please. Now, why he couldn't see Moses instead, I don't know. But then, Jews are not prone to visions, as you know. Christians, on the other hand, seem to see Jesus and Mary everywhere."

"Hey," he continued, raising his hands. "That's okay by me, only they should see him someplace other than in a synagogue in Washington Heights." Again the room filled with argument, his meager attempt at humor no longer placating his audience.

"However, a Christian didn't see Jesus in the shule. A nice Jewish boy did," he continued. The room roared with disapproval.

"Please, gentlemen, please," Stan pleaded, as he tapped the mike repeatedly. "Gentlemen, let me make this perfectly clear.

Hear my words. Sammy Levitt, the bar mitzvah in question, did not see a vision. He simply saw a pattern on a door that reminded him of a face he's seen in books and magazines all his life. Unfortunately he told this news to a priest instead of a rabbi, and so here we are. This kind of thing is a common occurrence. Awhile back someone saw a vision of Jesus in a bowl of pasta."

An old rabbi sitting along the wall next to two men overheard bits of the speech. He had a long white beard with a smattering of yellow in it, which made it look dirty. Large amounts of dandruff peppered his black coat. He pulled on the sleeve of the man closest to him and in a thick east European accent asked, "Voos ist doos pasta?"

The man looked down and smiled and said, "Pasta? Pasta is spaghetti."

"Spaghetti?"

"Yes. You know, spaghetti." The old man smiled a bit and nodded as if to thank him and he turned his attention back to Stan. Then a moment later he tugged on the man's sleeve again.

"Vot did he see in spaghetti?"

The man leaned down. "Jesus. He saw Jesus in a bowl of spaghetti."

The old man pulled at the sleeve again.

"So tell me, vhere you read this?"

"In the newspaper."

"Newspaper," the old man repeated, nodding his head, pondering.

"How can it be in spaghetti?"

"I don't know, Rabbi," the man said, a bit annoyed, trying to hear Stan. "It might have been on the bowl. Maybe in the sauce."

"Sauce? Jesus in the sauce?"

"Do you want to know what kind of sauce? Marinara. Maybe a clam sauce."

A man who was listening leaned over, clearly enjoying this. "Meatballs may have been involved."

The rabbi leaned back, nodding his head in thought, looking almost as if he were praying.

"I have been in touch with Bishop John Sticker, and he assures me that everything will be done to expiate this matter," Stan continued.

"What do we tell our congregations?" someone asked. The voices rose again.

"Tell them what I've told you, but please—and I can't emphasize this too much—please try not to make too much of this thing, and maybe it will all go away." Stan looked at the room, wondering if anyone really believed him.

"What about the parents?" someone shouted.

Stan continued to field questions. He explained that the parents were middle-class, hardworking people, like anyone in their congregation. The father was a manufacturer in the fur market, and the wife a homemaker. They had two boys, Sammy being the youngest.

"Please, gentlemen. I will visit the parents," Stan continued. "This is not the end of the world." Someone uttered in a voice that carried, "Maybe not yours, but what about the rabbi on Fort Washington Avenue?"

Stan nodded in resignation. He could say nothing more.

9

Sammy finished his breakfast and put on his windbreaker.
"Your toast," his mother said. "Finish your toast, Sammy."

"Aw, Ma, I'm not hungry."

"You will be in one hour. You didn't eat anything." She reached for the toast and wrapped it in wax paper. "Take it for later. Be a good boy."

Sammy put the toast in his pocket, kissed his mother, and headed for school. As the door closed behind him, he heard the phone ring. He couldn't remember the phone ever ringing in the house that early before. As he walked down the hall, he took the toast from his pocket and formed it into a ball. Then he pushed the button for the elevator. Behind him was the hall light about six feet from the floor, shaped like a half shell and covered with a smoky glass. Sammy looked at the indicator above the elevator doors. It showed the doors would open in about ten seconds. He faked left, then right, imitated a dribble and jump shot, the toast arcing with his hand as he thought of Tom Gola.

As the doors of the elevator closed he heard his mother calling him, but he couldn't catch them in time so he let them go, and whatever she had to offer, he still wasn't hungry.

When he entered school that morning, things felt different. Two girls saw him, smiled at each other, and whispered. It made him feel good.

But he was late. Even the school monitors at the traffic lights had left, and he hated walking into school after class had begun. Everyone would notice when he entered, and he didn't enjoy being noticed, except by girls.

He listened at the door of the classroom. By the noise he could tell that the class hadn't started. He opened the door and the room grew quiet. He placed his small briefcase under the desk as he took a seat. After he'd placed his notebook down, he looked to see what was happening, what books were open.

He caught the eye of one student. Sammy smiled, and was surprised that nothing was returned, but thought nothing of it.

"Where are we?" Sammy asked the girl next to him.

"We haven't started yet."

"Oh." This made sense to him. He hadn't thought the class had begun, but then it had grown quiet so quickly after he'd entered. He opened his notebook to review his homework. He wasn't sure of the answers, and he hoped the teacher wouldn't ask for them.

The door opened and the principal poked in her head, motioning Miss Cannon to come into the hallway. Having Miss Cannon out of the class for a moment excited him. It was like a fire drill—a few minutes of nothing. The class started to talk. Sammy continued to check his homework.

Miss Cannon returned and sat down at her desk. She glanced at the class and then placed her hand to her ear, feigning to listen intently.

"What's that noise?" she asked jokingly. "Ahh, silence," she sighed.

"Well, today will be a little different, class. As you know, soon you will be entering high school and approaching the day when you will make one of those life decisions—what you want to be. Where will you go and for what? Will you go to Stuyvesant, or Bronx Science, or Music and Art? Do you want to be a teacher or a doctor? What profession have you been thinking about? Not everyone knows what they want to be when they're thirteen years old. But if you do, it's a great head-start in life. So I will go around and ask each of you what you want to be, and you will stand up and tell the class and we will discuss it. Okay? Is that understood? Any questions?"

Sammy's heart soared. There would be no math today. Just talk. It was like having a substitute, his favorite kind of teacher. Usually a substitute would come when a teacher was ill, hand out paper to draw on, and require nothing but silence. Only going to the bathroom was allowed. He could just relax and sketch. He would start out with a car usually, trying to design a new chrome sideline he could see only in his head. That's where it stayed—Sammy couldn't draw well. But he liked the idea of designing the car of the future. After that, Sammy would just write out the lineups of the sixteen baseball teams, which he knew by heart, except for the Washington Senators, which were the worst. Or he would fold his arms on the desk, rest his head, and look out the window. It didn't matter. The substitute—and it usually was the same one—hardly ever looked up. She merely read the newspaper.

Miss Cannon began with the student nearest the door and proceeded down each row. It would be a long time before she got to Sammy, and he leaned back and relaxed. He thought about how he would answer. He had no idea what he wanted to be. He had never thought of it, or at least he couldn't remember if he had. His father was in the fur business. Perhaps that would be okay. Come to think of it, he had always thought he would be in a business of some sort. It was only natural. It was what Manny and his dad always talked about at the dinner table. That's it, Sammy thought. He'd say that he'd go into the fur business. He felt even more relaxed.

Students rattled off their choices in careers and schools. Time passed quickly. Sammy was actually enjoying himself. He couldn't remember ever being in Miss Cannon's class and not having fear.

Listening to his classmates talking about their career choices was interesting. He had never heard of an industrial engineer or an interior decorator—two of the more interesting jobs, he thought. Most kids talked about being a nurse or a lawyer, jobs he knew.

Sammy looked around. He felt free now to make eye contact with the other students, even with the teacher. He noticed a note being passed around, and a few kids snickering. He waited for it to get to him. Notes were the only form of freedom in a classroom. Soon he felt a tap on his shoulder and the pressure of a note stuck under his buttock. He looked at the teacher, then slowly brought the note up to his desktop. He looked up. A great number of his classmates were looking at him, and it bolstered his performance with the piece of paper. "What is the story of Easter?" it read. "Jesus came out of his cave, saw his shadow, and went back inside for six more weeks." He laughed to himself, smiled to show the audience his enjoyment, and passed the note on. He was still enjoying the moment when Miss Cannon called on him.

"What do you want to be, Mr. Levitt?"

Sammy thought for a second and heard someone behind him say in a somewhat hushed voice, "A priest." The back of the class stifled laughter.

"What's going on here?" Miss Cannon yelled, quieting the class. Then she turned her attention to Sammy.

"Mr. Levitt?"

Sammy stood up and said, "I would like to be an architect."

Miss Cannon's eyes lit up.

"An architect," she said, almost playfully. "And why would you want to be an architect?"

Then he froze. Why did he want to be an architect? He had just heard someone say architect. The blood drained from his face. All he could think about was why he hadn't said he wanted to be a furrier instead.

"Mr. Levitt," Miss Cannon continued suspiciously, "what does an architect do?"

Sammy stood there as if he'd been asked to describe the theory of relativity. He looked at Miss Cannon, unable to answer, as her expression turned to disgust. How had he done this? he asked himself.

Behind him he could hear snickering.

"Sit down, Mr. Levitt," Miss Cannon said in disgust.

Sammy did as he was told, then stared at his notebook so as not to have to look at anyone else. He thought of Lyn across the room. He didn't dare raise his head.

He felt a piece of paper behind him again and reached for it. Another joke. For a moment he was relieved. Inclusion—a part of being accepted. He passed it slowly across his lap, opened it, and looked down. It was a newspaper clipping. His eyes fixed at the title and he could feel a smile on his face at the recognition and wondered for a second why he was smiling, for his heart was racing now, and he was scared. On his lap was a short article about Sammy Levitt, a Jewish boy in Washington Heights who saw a vision of Jesus. He couldn't look up. He couldn't move, and he was afraid to keep his head down. My God! he thought. My parents! My mother and father! He thought about going to the bathroom but couldn't bear to stand up. If he could have, the torture would have ended much sooner. He could leave school.

It was an eternity before the bell rang for classes to change. Chairs pushed back. Books slammed shut, making those welcome sounds of conclusion. Sammy sat while the class left the room. Then he walked out, looking for the closest exit. Some kids laughed and pointed, but he could hardly make them out, his eyes bleary with tears. Down the stairs he ran, books in hand.

Then it struck him. Gym class was next. That meant Bombardment, a game like dodgeball, which the entire class played. It was one of his favorite school activities. He wouldn't just leave.

10

The seventh-grade class was divided into two teams on the gymnasium floor, separated by the half-court. The boys and girls were mixed and neither team had a clear advantage. The boys moved around strategically, eyeing the players on the other team who possessed a ball. Four or five balls were always in play. The ball was red and soft to the touch, about half the size of a basketball. Being hit by one didn't hurt even if thrown with full force.

The rules were simple. If a player got hit with a ball, he or she was out. If a player caught the ball on the fly, the thrower was out. Early in the game, the court was packed with so many kids it was like shooting fish in a barrel. The better athletes tried to catch the ball and ceremoniously were handed it to throw at the enemy. Many balls were used, so balls were usually bouncing about and could easily roll up and just touch the back of an unsuspecting shoe, and he or she was out. The girls clung together, screaming in fear or laughing hysterically as the boys aimed at crushing them. When hit, the girls exited the game gleefully, then spent the rest of the time laughing on the sidelines while they rooted for their team. It was dodgeball, only at P.S. 187 it was called "Bombardment."

Sammy hung back and watched carefully. He picked up a loose ball and approached the half-court. Out of his right eye he caught sight of Barry about to throw his ball. It came straight for Sammy's head, and Sammy lifted his ball and blocked it. If he had dropped his ball, he would have been out. Sammy pivoted and threw at a small group of players on the other side; one girl ran off the court. Gym class was a little less than an hour, and it took about thirty minutes to thin out the crowd. Soon enough, the hour was winding down, and Sammy found himself standing with a boy and two girls. Standing alone was always exciting. All the attention was on the remaining player, and that player's team would cheer him or her on and warn of incoming balls.

Sammy picked up one ball after another and kept throwing, and finally found himself alone, opposite a few on the other side. Only there were no cheers for him. Everyone seemed to be cheering for the other team to cream him. He couldn't figure out why, as he held a ball near his chest for protection. He couldn't beat these guys, he thought, but if he could deflect throws until the bell rang, that would be a kind of victory. His eyes kept darting to the floor, looking for loose balls rolling around and at the same time eyeing Barry and Jesse, who could wipe him out if he wasn't careful. And there were always those loose balls rolling around. Many a great athlete was kicked out because he didn't notice a loose ball rolling his way.

Rod walked up to Barry, who called over Jesse and mapped out a strategy. They split up. Jesse rolled his ball slowly toward Sammy. Sammy watched it and moved away; Rod let loose a bullet, followed by one from Barry from a different direction. It was perfect. Sammy ducked from one ball and got hit by another, losing control of his own ball. The game was over. The entire class cheered, but not for Sammy. He looked up and got hit in the ear by a ball, and then another that followed. An eerie sound in his head blocked out the laughter, though he could see it in his classmates' faces. The students piled out of the gym, heading toward the next class as Sammy stood there. Soon, he was alone with the gym teacher, picking up the balls.

"Shouldn't you get to class, son?" the teacher asked.

He nodded, walked to the edge of the court, picked up his books, and walked out. But he didn't go to the next class. He left school and headed home. His face felt flush when he thought of the newspaper clipping. His name was mentioned. He saw it. Why else would everyone be after me? he thought. Then he wondered why Shelley hadn't said something. Shelley was just the same. Shelley hadn't talked to him much lately, and he wondered why. Was it coincidental?

He wanted to run, but he didn't want to draw attention to himself. He walked deliberately, counting steps. Each step brought him closer to his apartment building. Five hundred more steps, he told himself. Then 400. He thought about the game and how the class had cheered when he dropped the ball. Normally a groan would have been unleashed as the underdog failed against Barry and Jesse, two of the best athletes in the class. Instead the class had cheered, and he'd stood there like a bowling pin amid the balls rolling around the floor. He played back the scene, saw himself holding to the ball and thereby not losing. He wondered what the reaction would have been. Would they have cheered? They hated him now, and that scared him. He wanted to go home and hug his mother.

He crossed the street, continuing the count. Over 300 steps already. It would probably be 600 or more. As he saw his building in the distance, he felt relief, but then he slowed. He thought about his mom and pictured the phone off the hook.

He went into the building, took the elevator down, and placed his books in the bicycle room. He slinked out the back door, walked behind the 730 building, and headed for the park. Only grown-ups walked in the park.

He walked past the basketball courts. No one was shooting hoops. Too early. Then he crossed the circle and entered Fort Tryon Park. From the entrance he could see all the way to the

Cloisters monastery, nearly a quarter of a mile away. No one was in sight except a park man sweeping trash. Except for the occasional tour bus, the park was not visited by people other than those from the neighborhood. During the week it was bare, the squirrels outnumbering the people.

For Sammy the park wasn't a place to play. It was more a place to hide or walk with his father and mother after dinner. The only time he ran to the park was when it snowed, for that was where Suicide Hill was, and it was there that he'd find everyone with sleds. The park had no ballfields in which to play baseball or football. For that he'd have had to go to Inwood, a great distance away for a kid. Fort Tryon was a pedestrian park. People avoided walking on the grass, as directed. The flowers were undisturbed. In the evening it was a little like Europe, as German Jews from the neighborhood walked the main promenade aimed toward the Cloisters or occupied its wooden benches.

With his hands in his pockets Sammy waded through pigeons, bobbing their heads, inspecting peanuts, shells, and trash, discarded by patrons from the benches nearby. The pigeons flapped their wings to get away, rising only a foot in the air, being accustomed to people. Ahead of him Sammy glimpsed Matt, headed for the park. Sammy warmed at the sight of him. Though they weren't really friends, he wanted to see him and talk to him. He thought about the card-flipping and hoped Matt didn't know anything of the trouble he was in. Sammy looked at him as he would a close friend, even though he knew he wasn't. But could he be a close friend now? he wondered. There was a sense of relief in knowing that, at the very least, he could enjoy the illusion of having a friend.

"Matt!" Sammy called out. "Matt!"

Matt turned.

"Sammy!"

"Why ain't you in school?" Sammy asked.

"Teacher conference day."

"What's that?"

"Teachers talk with the parents. It's a day off. What're you doin' here?" he asked, looking at his watch.

Sammy thought for a second. "Nothing, just hangin' out."

Matt thought for a second and took out two pieces of chalk from his pocket. "Wanna play Fox and Hounds?"

"Sure," Sammy answered, relieved at a question that felt so normal. He thought back to school. His stomach felt queasy. But he didn't want to go home yet.

"I'll be the fox," Matt offered.

"What are the rules?" Sammy asked, never having played before.

"You close your eyes, count to 1,000, and I run away. You try to find me by following the trail I leave." Matt held up one of the pieces of chalk. "Voila!"

"You can be the fox. And what are you doing with chalk in your pocket? Nobody carries chalk." Matt smiled. "You wanna play or not?"

"Yeah, I'll play but I ain't counting to 1,000. That's bullshit."

"Okay, just wait ten minutes."

"You can be in Jersey in ten minutes."

"FIVE minutes," he countered.

"Okay, go ahead. I'm closing my eyes," Sammy said. When Matt had run off, he muttered, "Yeah, right."

He placed his hand over his eyes, and when he could no longer hear Matt, he parted his fingers and watched him run, stopping every so often to write something on the ground. When Matt was out of sight, Sammy started after him at a brisk walk.

He'd left arrows, chalk arrows, on the pavement. Following the path was easy, until Sammy came to a fork and couldn't figure out which way to go. Then he noticed an arrow on a tree trunk. He was getting the hang of the game, and he was enjoying it. For a moment he wasn't thinking about school or the newspaper article.

After a few minutes he caught a glimpse of Matt and thought he was heading for the Cloisters. That made sense. He wondered whether he should head straight for Matt or follow the arrows. Would it be fair just to go after Matt without following the arrows? But Matt had bent down and marked the arrows, and it wouldn't be right to ignore them. Then he wished he hadn't peeked in the beginning. From here on, he wouldn't cut corners. He found himself walking, trotting, and smiling. It felt good to smile.

The arrows led to Suicide Hill. How strange to be here without snow, he thought, standing at the hill's edge. Everything looked so tame without a mob of kids sledding down on their bellies or backsides. It was faster to go on the belly because of the running start, but you always got snow in your face. A great ride could get you from the top of the hill to the entrance on Broadway below.

Sammy looked for an arrow, saw none, and sat down to catch his breath. Then he noticed a couple, midway down the hill, lying down on the grass. In the background he could hear the traffic of Broadway as it passed Jewish Memorial Hospital. He looked to see if anyone else was around, as if it wasn't right to watch, then he rested his chin on his knees. As he caught his breath he watched the couple grope each other. The couple was probably in high school, he thought. She was on her back and the boy was on his side, resting his head on his hand and leaning on his elbow. One moment they were kissing and laughing, and the next they were back at it, kissing. Sammy became excited. The boy was plying his trade as best he could. He would snake his hand beneath her blouse, and she would push it gently away. Then he kissed her and tried his hand again, and again and she would parry like a promising bantamweight. He lifted his leg over hers, and she rose and pushed it away, looking around as if she were embarrassed. She almost looked Sammy's way, and he turned his face to the left, as if he was admiring the scenery.

When he looked back, they were kissing again. He wished the boy were him, and he thought of Lyn again. She was so pretty. He imagined kissing this girl now and bringing her home. His nose twitched, thinking of the reception she would receive. His family wouldn't approve. He knew that. "But I love her," he would say, and he would hope that they would understand, like Robert Young in "Father Knows Best," where parents always know just what to say.

The girl placed her arms around the boy's neck and brought him closer to her. Sammy felt a rush. How good that must feel to be kissed and held like that. Did she have a brassiere on? How did that feel? He felt himself getting hard. He couldn't see their faces, but they were dark-skinned, and he imagined the girl as pretty and wished he had a girlfriend like her. The boy kissed her neck and placed his hand on the top button of her blouse, and as he did she rolled him over and lay on top of him, kissing him hard. Sammy noticed grass on her back and imagined brushing it off, then placing his hand under her blouse, as the young man was now doing.

Again they rolled. The girl's blouse was loose. Sammy's heart was racing. He looked around. He marveled at how they were kissing in the middle of the field, not in the bushes. He stood up, then, feeling the bulge in his pants, sat back down. Soon after, though, the couple stopped kissing, rolled onto their backs, and stared into the sky.

Sammy thought of Matt. He wondered how long he'd been sitting there. He felt his nose twitch, got up, and began walking toward the Cloisters again until he picked up an arrow. He glanced back at the couple and that good feeling came over him again, and he liked it.

At a fork, an arrow pointed Sammy left to the park restaurant. He stopped. Sammy loved this small eatery, built of the same granite lining the walkways of the park. Sammy often imagined having a piece of cake there. Capped with a slate roof, it had the appearance of Robert Burns's "Alloway," only three times the size and with normal-sized windows. It looked like those small stone restaurants on the Saw Mill River Parkway that Sammy's family would pass when traveling north.

A line of arrows led to the restaurant's front entrance. Sammy followed them. He expected a sharp arrow directing him around the building. Instead, at the entrance he found an arrow pointing up. He wondered whether he'd find Matt inside drinking a Coke, whether the game was over. He imagined Matt slyly making arrows inside when no one was looking.

Sammy pushed through the door and examined the interior, much as a tourist might. He imagined all eyes upon him, but no one noticed as he looked around for an arrow. A small one on the stone floor directed him toward the food line. He smiled at the lady behind the counter. It was past lunchtime, and he was hungry. He placed his hand in his right pocket and counted about twenty cents. He looked at the menu on the wall. A grilled cheese was seventy-five cents. His allowance was thirty-five cents a week. He wouldn't have enough even for cake and coffee. Just coffee, he thought. He walked along the outside of the serving line, gazing at the ceiling as if it were the Sistine Chapel. An arrow on the cash register directed him to the seating area. He examined the floor, figuring that would be the only place an arrow could be now. The lady at the counter looked at him quizzically.

Another arrow led him past a table where two park men in green jackets were sipping coffee and talking. The one with his back to Sammy had a headless arrow on his back pointing either to his head or to the crack in his ass.

Then he caught sight of the arrow on the wall. It pointed towards the restroom. On the door was the nameplate: "Ladies' Room." My God, Sammy thought. Panic seized him. Then he realized he didn't have to go in there. He could walk outside and see where the arrows picked up again. But what if there were no arrows outside, just a direction in the bathroom sending him to another location?

Sammy leaned against the wall, glancing at the counter lady and then at a cleaning man at the other end of the restaurant, mopping the floor, making his way toward him. When he was sure they weren't looking, he pressed against the door and went inside.

For a moment he stood frozen, waiting for someone to come after him, but no one did. Arrows pointed to a stall, and he walked inside and locked the stall door behind him. Competing with the graffiti was a bold message from Matt: "Congratulations for having the balls to follow me here. If I don't see you by the flagpole in a few minutes, I will know you have cheated. Arrows continue there. Love always, Matt."

Sammy smiled at the humor. He felt glad, almost happy, that he came into the ladies' room.

There was a "p.s.": "Leave through the window. It was a bitch to open, and you won't get busted leaving the ladies' room."

He was about to open the stall door and exit when he heard the bathroom door open. Someone walked in and came to one of the sinks. A lady grooming herself, he thought. He slowly closed the lock on the stall and sat down, trying not to make any noise. Then he realized that he didn't have to be quiet. Better someone think the stall is occupied, he thought. He faked a cough. The woman opened the stall door next to him and sat on the toilet, humming a bit.

"Lord, a'mercy!" she said after a while. There was a splash. Sammy stifled a laugh. "Lord, a'mighty!" There was another splash.

Sammy could not control his laughter. He tried coughing, but only made mucous come out of his nose. Then he flushed the toilet and sat there hoping she would leave first, and then she finally finished and left.

Sammy opened the stall door and looked at himself in the mirror. His nose twitched, exposing the gap in his teeth. "Ugly," he thought, and wished he could stop.

He looked at the bathroom door. He didn't want to exit through the window. He thought of Lemon, a guy in the neighborhood who walked backwards through the exit doors of the RKO as patrons left so that no one would notice as he inched into the theater for free. But that wouldn't work in this situation. There was no crowd. So Sammy opened the window, stepped on the radiator, peeked out the window, and jumped.

The flagpole sits at the highest point of Fort Tryon Park. From there one can get a wide view of the Hudson River, north toward West Point. But the main object of one's attention would be the Cloisters, a medieval monastery resting on a knoll just a few hundred yards away. Sammy assumed that Matt would be headed there, but an arrow on the pole led to another arrow, and another, and he found himself down the hill at the Riverside

Drive entrance, heading away from the monastery. He stood on the white line separating the lanes of the road, looking for an arrow. Before him, on each side, was a towering stone wall next to the archway for cars to pass. Then he saw the next arrow, and the next, and unbelievably, the next. Matt had somehow scaled the north wall, making short little chalk marks toward the top. Sammy stood amazed. Only a salamander could climb a wall like this, he thought, but it fit Matt's personality perfectly. A car's horn sounded and Sammy scurried toward the wall, looking up. It looked worse up close. Then he searched for Matt, wondering if he was watching.

At first glance the wall seemed as difficult to climb as one of new brick. But the granite stones were irregular, and there was wiggle-room for the toe portion of the shoe. If Matt had scaled the wall, that meant that Sammy could do it, too. All he had to do was follow the arrows. He wondered if Matt had put the chalk in his mouth or used one of his hands to write. Was Matt right-handed, or left? Sammy didn't know. He looked for freshly moved earth between the stones, anything. He placed his foot in a spot and straightened up. His head was to one side, and he found himself hugging the wall like a fly. This is bullshit, he thought. He looked up and then looked down for another place to step. Nothing. Then he looked to his left for a place to grab. "He's a lefty," Sammy muttered. He jumped down and looked at the wall again. Now he could see some fresh movement to the right of the arrows and began again.

"If he could do it, I can," he repeated to himself. A chill was in the air as clouds covered the sun. He looked to the top of the wall. It was about twenty feet. He stuck his toe in the first spot he could find. He looked for a new place to grip. His face rubbed the cold stone. His windbreaker flapped in the wind, distracting him. Below, a car drove by, and another. He felt embarrassed.

How foolish he must look up here, a lone kid climbing a stupid wall! For what? He grabbed the top of a new stone above him and pulled himself up, looking for a place to stick his foot. When he found that, he saw that his nose was touching an arrow. He was halfway now and feeling better. I can do this, he thought. He saw another place to grab but couldn't reach it. Matt was taller. He stretched with one foot still in a groove on tiptoe, reached, and slipped. One foot dangled. Shit—the hell with it! he cursed silently. He looked down and he was scared. It was too high to jump, and it would be harder to go back down now. He looked left and then right. He couldn't follow Matt, so he decided to make his own way. He grabbed a stone to his left and made a modest gain towards the top. He found himself nose-to-nose with a flower. It wasn't a daisy or a dandelion, and he knew only a few flowers: roses, tulips, and his favorite, lilacs. He felt like a Lilliputian. The flower was staring him in the eye like a redwood. By now the occasional car below sounded far away. Just a few more feet and he would be there. He was feeling really good about climbing the wall. No one would believe him, though.

Finally his fingers touched the top of the last stone. He stretched farther and felt grass. One or two more footholds and he would be there. Don't look down. He saw a spot but he couldn't lift his leg high enough, and stood for a while with the left side of his face against the stone. Then he placed his other hand on top of what felt like a ledge and pulled himself up, both feet dangling in the air. One of his hands began to lose its grip, the dirt too loose, and he frantically looked for a spot to place a foot as he pulled his body up to reach it. He jabbed his toe into the only place he could find. It held. Then he pushed on it and rose, putting his chest over the top.

He lay there breathing hard for a moment, but was elated he made it. After a while he crawled the rest of the way up the grass, turned around, and laid on his back looking at the darkening sky. He turned and looked over the edge. The cars indeed did appear smaller. The corresponding wall across the street mirrored what he had just scaled. He hadn't felt this good in a long time. He thought about telling some friends, but then he realized that they wouldn't care and wouldn't believe him. Thoughts of the morning came rushing in again, and his nose twitched. He climbed over a short, stone retaining wall, landing in front of an old lady, who was clearly startled.

"You crazy or sometink?" she yelled in a Jewish accent. Sammy raised his hands in mock surrender. "Enshuldigmeer," he said in Yiddish and gingerly walked away. He wondered if the Cloisters would still be open. The day had raced by and so much had happened. He thought back to the couple on Suicide Hill and the restaurant and the stone wall. It all was so different for him and so surprisingly good. He caught an arrow on one of the benches pointing toward the Cloisters and headed straight toward the main entrance, on the north side of the building.

To Sammy, the Cloisters was a castle, only it wasn't a play castle. There were guards, but only a few, to look after the art that lined the walls and hallways. The road immediately in front of the entrance was made of old Belgian blocks, which caused cars to slow down considerably as they passed over them. To some it was one of the best-kept secrets in New York City. The neighborhood thought of it as its own, when in fact it was a part of the Metropolitan Museum of Art, bequeathed by the Rockefellers, who donated the land, purchased the artifacts from George Grey Barnard, an American sculptor, and commenced building it from scratch in 1934, using architectural pieces from five different French monasteries, and completing it in 1938. Most thought it was one monastery taken apart stone by stone and transported to America.

Sammy thought that by placing one hand in his pants pocket he would look like a tourist and not attract too much attention. There was no air conditioning, but the stone walls kept the building cool. Sammy walked past the large wooden door and noted its thickness. He thought of his own apartment door and the solid sound it made as it clicked shut. It was a metal door painted forest green. He wondered how this door sounded. He imagined there was no clicking sound. Rather, a thud or a clunk.

He passed a monk dressed in a brown robe, with a tan rope tied around as a belt, as he headed toward the Fuentiduena Chapel, which rose two stories and whose large candles kept it well lit. A couple of arrows had pointed him this way, and he stood there as if admiring the architecture but only looking for more arrows.

As he walked through the entrance, he was taken by how cool it was. It was getting colder outside, yet it was still cooler inside, just like in the summer. Admission was free, and he often came here at that time of year. Few people ventured to the Cloisters, except during the weekends, when tour buses appeared from great distances.

An arrow on the floor pointed toward a walkway lined with Belgian tapestries. Sammy walked slowly, noticing the wall hangings for the first time. He stopped in front of one, backed up, and sat down to examine it. The characters were too stiff, marching like wooden soldiers. He wondered how old it was. Then he thought of his bar mitzvah, and a sick feeling came to his stomach. He thought of his haftorah. Did he know it? Yes, he thought. And his speech, did he know that? His nose twitched again. He was beginning to rehearse the speech in his head, when he saw a shadow. He didn't move as the shadow came closer.

"Who's better, Mantle or Mays?" said a voice. A young man in one of those brown cloth garments stood next to Sammy, smiling.

"Duke," Sammy answered. The man reminded him of Little John from *Robin Hood.*

The man laughed. "A Dodger fan? Snider had a great year."

"Almost won the batting title."

"That's right. Who won it in the end, Mueller or Mays?"

"Mays," Sammy said with a frown.

"Mays is a great ballplayer, but I don't think you like Mays."

"He's great and all, but he's a Giant. I hate the Giants," Sammy said, his nose twitching. The man was young. Not much older than Manny, he thought. Then he wondered, why don't I think of Manny as a "man"?

"Did you see Mueller hit that single when he was supposed to be taking an intentional walk?"

"I did!"

"Was that crazy or what?"

"He got fined for that, you know," Sammy said.

"Yeah, but I bet he felt it was worth it. He just stuck his bat out there and smacked it into shallow leftfield. I never saw that before, ever. Do you live in the neighborhood? What's your name?"

"Sammy..." He wanted to say "Levitt" but decided against it. No need to tell him he was Jewish.

"I'm John Albert."

"A priest?"

John Albert laughed. "No, not yet."

Sammy smiled at him. He wanted to know if he was a monk but didn't want to ask.

"What is a monastery? Is it a church or something?"

"Think of it as a place of study. Come with me. I'll show you around."

"Aren't you closing?"

"I know the boss." He winked. "C'mon."

Sammy thought about similar institutions in Judaism and could only come up with a Yeshiva. That was for students. "So it's not for students?"

"Well, in a way we're all students, but not in a classical sense."

Sammy felt like he was in a very safe place, like being inside of something looking out. If anyone else was in the building, he could hardly tell. As they walked up the cold, gray stone stairs, Sammy looked up, taking in the stone arches. John Albert pointed out some of the tapestries.

"I heard that Rockefeller owned this place," Sammy said.

"He did. In fact, he inspired it. I think it is the only thing like it in the country."

Sammy's eyes widened. He smiled at John Albert. Then his nose twitched, and he turned his face to hide it.

John Albert put his arm around him and walked him into the interior courtyard. "Peaceful, isn't it?"

"Yeah, but the whole park is peaceful," Sammy said.

"You're right. It's a beautiful park." They sat in silence on a stone bench.

"Do you have any siblings?"

"Siblings?"

"Brothers or sisters."

"I have an older brother—Manny. He's a comedian."

"A comedian. Wow! A real comedian?"

"Well, not one on TV, but he does shows at college and stuff."

"That's pretty impressive. Do you think he's funny?"

"He's a riot. He's always making me laugh. One time my dad threw beer in his face. He didn't think it was so funny."

"Wow! That must have been serious."

"Yeah, I guess. All I remember was not being able to stop laughing."

"Some things are funny to some and not so funny to others."

"Yeah," Sammy said, and then, realizing that it was getting late, said, "I gotta go."

"I'll show you out."

As they re-entered the building and walked slowly down the hall, Sammy thought about his day at school and worried about his bar mitzvah.

He looked at the brown robe that covered the man next to him—the man with the soft, gentle manner who had taught him a bit of the world he never knew. He felt like he could tell him all his secrets and they would never leave this place. He wanted to grab his arm and relax with him like a kid brother, and not have to leave. It was like that feeling he had of wanting to be in a prison cell, playing his baseball game, left to roll the dice and just play. Not see anyone. Just to roll the dice and keep statistics and be safe.

"Can I come again and see you, maybe?"

John Albert looked at him. "Are you okay?"

"Yeah, I'm okay."

"You're sure?" John Albert asked.

"I don't want to confess or anything."

John Albert laughed.

"Just wondering. You can come back anytime and ask for me if you like."

"Great. Thanks."

And with that, Sammy trotted outside, thinking to himself that he would come back the next day. As he walked home, he imagined Matt already eating dinner with his family.

11

Sammy could tell something was different the moment he opened the door to his apartment. He saw his father place a shot glass down on the shelf over the small cabinet along the dining room wall that served as a bar. His father refilled the glass. Two shots. He'd never seen his father take two shots. Normally, after one shot he would give out a sigh, and if Sammy was around, he would smile. Once, when Sammy asked about drinking so much, his father laughed and explained the joy of taking a shot: how it made you feel, and that taking a shot was not "drinking so much." "Ten shots" was "drinking too much." But he didn't sigh this time.

Sammy was sure his father had heard him come in. That metal door could be heard from any room in the apartment. But he didn't turn around. He just looked at himself in the split mirror in front of him and removed his hat.

Manny came around the corner from the bedroom, and as he passed his father, he said hello, saw Sammy, and made a gesture to him as if slitting his throat. Sammy's heart began to pound and he walked into the kitchen instead of approaching his father. His mother was standing near the stove, saw him, and pointed her finger to his chair. Sammy sat and stared at the table. He was scared now, scared as he had ever been. More scared than when he took a chance by not telling his mother to come to school as requested by the teacher because of his bad behavior one day. Manny walked by and, with a spoon, took a sample from a pot on the stove.

"Here, I'll fix you a bowl," his mother said.

"I can wait."

"You don't have to wait."

"It's okay. Dad's ready, I think," Manny said.

Sammy wished he was having that conversation, not Manny. He wished that dinner would run like other nights. Minutes later, his father came to the table and sat down. Though it was unthinkable, he didn't acknowledge Sammy. Sammy looked at the cold, marinated, chopped eggplant before him. When his mother sat down, she nudged him to eat. Sammy picked up a fork and picked at the eggplant, a dish he had just recently begun to acquire a taste for. He placed a bite in his mouth but stared at the plate as he ate. He dared not look at his father. The lemony taste was foreign to anything else he ever put in his mouth, and he loved it. He looked at his mother, and she smiled, but her smile was tentative, and he became nervous. He stuck his fork in again, wanting to disappear. He could not remember a dinner without talk. The sounds of knives and forks against plates became louder as the silence grew. He noticed the phone was off the hook.

Sammy's mother got up and cleared the plates but left Sammy's, pushing it aside to make room for the bowl of split-pea soup that came as the next course. Sammy began to feel as he did when he was scolded in class. The sounds of the outside world faded, and the other sounds close to him amplified until he felt as if he was in a bubble.

"HOW COULD YOU DO THIS?" Sid suddenly blurted out, looking directly at him. Sammy's eyes welled up, and he blinked to stop the flow. His nose twitched.

"AND STOP WITH YOUR NOSE, FOR GOD'S SAKE!"

"Sid!" Sammy's mother pleaded.

"WELL?"

He knew what his father was referring to, but he was afraid to answer. "Do what?" he asked softly.

"Jesus, Sammy? Jesus! For Christ's sake!" Manny shouted, and turned away to avoid laughing.

Sid got up and walked to the foyer and brought back the *Post.* "Here!" he said, slapping his hand on the folded newspaper. Sammy looked at the paper on the table but not at his father. Sid took the paper away and threw it on the floor. Sammy's mother sat at the table holding her napkin to her chin with both hands, as if paralyzed. Sid shook his head slowly. "I don't know where to begin. Idyot you," he said in a controlled voice. The expression his father used instead of "you idiot" normally provoked laughter from his sons, but Sammy dared not laugh this time.

"WELL?! JESUS?! YOU SAW JESUS?! I CAN'T BELIEVE I'M SAYING IT!"

"I didn't see Jesus," Sammy mumbled.

"What? I can't hear you."

"I said I didn't see Jesus."

Sid picked up the newspaper and showed it to him. "Then what's this, Chinese? This says you saw Jesus. Here in the paper. The whole world knows my bar mitzvah boy sees Jesus. You couldn't see Moses?"

"Well, at least he didn't see Allah," Manny quipped.

"MANNY!" his mother shouted.

Sammy stared at his plate, blinking his eyes to hold back tears. He looked at the soup and counted the frankfurter slices floating in the bowl. Four. He loved this soup, but he wasn't sure he should eat while being yelled at. He looked at his mother, and she placed her hand on his head and caressed his face, arriving at his chin and raising it. "Blow on it. Eat." Sammy took his first sip.

"Did you think about the rabbi? What it would do to him?" Sid asked.

Obviously not, he wanted to say, but held back. "I didn't think," he said.

"No, you didn't. I got phone calls at work," he said, looking at Mara. "I thought it was business, and it was mishugas. Unbelievable! My son here to be bar-mitzvahed soon, and he sees Jesus! Look at our phone. We can't even use it."

"Dad, I—"

"Please. Don't say anything right now. Eat your dinner. Everybody, eat. It's good, Mara," Sid said to his wife, almost apologetically.

The rest of the meal was eaten in silence. Sammy could hear himself chew and wondered if it was as loud to the table as it was to him. There was always talk at the table and he realized that he'd never heard himself eat.

Later he lay on his bed staring at the light bulb. He heard the front door close and watched as his model planes, dangling from the ceiling, swayed in response. His father was going to the incinerator with the garbage, Sammy thought. But then he remembered that his father didn't normally close the door for that. When he didn't return, Sammy went to the kitchen.

"Mom, where's Dad?"

"He said he was going for a walk."

"What for?"

"What do you mean, 'what for'? He's going for a walk."

Sammy went to the closet and grabbed his windbreaker. "I'm gonna catch up with Dad," he told his mom before she could say anything.

When he got to the sidewalk, he looked right toward the park, but it was dark, and his father wouldn't have walked in the dark. Besides, the park was closed after sunset—or so the newly placed sign said. Until recently it had been open all night, but lately things had changed. Crime had come to the neighborhood, and there was much talk of it: whose apartment had been robbed or who got mugged near the train station.

He looked left towards 187th Street and saw what he thought was his father's hat. He ran toward him, slowing as he recognized his father's easy gait. His father might still be angry at him or at the whole situation he had caused. Sammy didn't want to anger him more so he walked slowly, but for Sammy "slow" was still too fast, so he began to serpentine. He wondered where his father was going. Maybe to the bakery or the drug store or Stein's candy store. Everything else was closed, except the little grocery.

When his father reached 187th Street, he would have to look both ways before crossing, Sammy thought, so he hid behind a tree, stepping in dog shit. "Aw, shit," he said. Sid didn't stop. He continued walking toward 184th. Sammy became nervous. He scraped the shit from his shoe onto the curb and began walking toward his father. Where's he going? The newsstand, that's it. The newsstand at 184th had everything, but his dad only went to the newsstand on Saturday night once in a while to get the Sunday paper. Maybe this was a special occasion. Maybe he wanted to see what the morning paper had to say.

Sammy lost his father as he approached the newsstand. People were exiting the subway station, and Sammy had to inch his way through the crowd, but it only grew more intense. He glanced around for his father and realized, then, that he was now in front of the synagogue. The people didn't look familiar. Some carried signs referring to "Sammy's sighting." Other signs boasted expressions concerning Jesus. Sammy looked at the synagogue doors to see if his father would enter, but a policeman was standing in front of them. Two men were building a makeshift platform out of two-by-fours and plywood. Sammy carved his way through the crowd and looked south. He caught a glimpse of his father's hat. Where's he going? Sammy wondered. It's Friday night! His father hardly ever walked to 181st Street. Sammy wanted to call out, but he was afraid. His father had seemed so angry. And then he caught a glimpse of the lights atop the George Washington Bridge, and in an instant, he figured it out. He's going to jump off the bridge, Sammy thought.

"No, please, no," he heard himself say in a low voice, running now. He was a block behind. I'll be good, he thought. Please don't jump. I'm sorry. I won't do anything bad again, I promise. You can't jump, please.

Sid was approaching the corner, and it looked to Sammy that if he headed straight, it would be too late, though the bridge was still three blocks away. No stores were in that direction. The only reason to go that way was to jump.

My father can't die, it isn't fair. Sammy hadn't thought of death this much since his first encounter with it years before in Brooklyn. He was at a friend's house, and as they walked through the main bedroom, his friend pointed to his mother's bed and said that his father died there. Sammy was seven, and when he looked at this place of sleep, it seemed both scary and mysterious—a feeling, perhaps, that he was not supposed to know. Since then he always thought of the color green when he thought of death. The bedroom had been green.

Now Sammy was looking at his father's back, and it was blurry, and Sammy realized that he was crying. Why couldn't I have seen Duke Snider instead of Jesus? he asked himself. Everyone would have laughed and made fun of me, but it wouldn't be like this.

He wiped his eyes with his sleeve and the salty taste of mucous touched his lips. He continued until his father stopped. Sammy stopped then as well but then continued. He wanted his father to see him. If he sees me, he won't jump, he thought.

"Dad, no!" he yelled, tripping over an uneven sidewalk and hitting the cement like he was stealing a base headfirst.

Sid turned and looked at Sammy sprawled on the sidewalk, his face up, crying and screaming. He edged toward his son.

"Sammy!" he said as he sat.

Sammy grabbed onto his father's waist, continuing to cry.

"Sammy," Sid said again, in a gentle voice. "What are you doing here?"

"I thought you were going to jump."

"Jump? Jump where?"

"The bridge," Sammy said.

"Jump off the George Washington Bridge?"

Sammy nodded, and Sid let out a big laugh and hugged him. At that moment, as he took in the smell of his father's jacket, Sammy forgot all his fears. After a minute passed, Sid placed his finger under Sammy's chin and raised it. "Let's see those hands," he said. "Looks okay, but we'll have to put iodine on them when we get home. And why would I jump off the bridge? Why would I do something so foolish?"

Sammy didn't answer.

"Huh? Come on now, tell me."

"Because of what we talked about—the Jesus thing."

"Oh, I see. Well, here, stand up and let's see what your clothes look like." He turned Sammy around. "Nothing for mom to get upset about."

They began walking down 181st Street toward Broadway.

"Don't worry, Sammy. I won't be jumping off any bridge. Not because of Jesus."

"Are you still angry?"

Sid thought for a second and then looked at Sammy.

"Yes, I am upset. I'm no longer angry, but I am upset. I don't know how this is going to get resolved. I don't know how to fix this. So I'm upset. But I'm no longer angry with you." And then he hugged Sammy. Sammy closed his eyes in his father's embrace and relaxed.

"Where were you going?" he asked

"The bank. It's open until eight. It's Friday."

"That's right!" Sammy said excitedly. His father wasn't going to jump. They walked together in silence as Sammy looked around at the stores that were still open, feeling good again.

They entered the Harlem Savings Bank from 181st Street. They passed a man polishing a brass rail, and Sammy marveled at the echo and the hushed sounds of feet on the marble floors and the voices of clerks talking to their customers. The sounds were not like those Sammy had heard in the stores. This was a serious place. Only a bank could make these sounds. It felt like the safest place in the world.

"Dad?"

"Yes."

"How could there be a Depression?"

Sid laughed. "What brought that on? Wait. We're next. I'll tell you in a minute." Sid took out his savings book and placed it on the counter. Sammy looked at the older woman behind the brass bars. She noticed him but didn't smile. Sammy dropped his.

When his father had finished his transaction, Sammy took hold of his big hand. They walked outside and headed up 181st Street toward home.

"So how could there be a Depression with all these big buildings?" Sammy asked.

"Well, it's hard to explain, but a depression doesn't come because of the buildings you have. It comes about when trust in one another breaks down or confidence in the economy is shaken."

"But these buildings are so solid."

"You mean the bank?"

"Yeah."

"Well, they build banks with marble and brass to make them look strong. It gives you confidence. If the bank looked like a shack, you might wonder about the strength of the bank. You might not want to put your money there."

"But it's so solid."

"Yes, it is solid, and we won't have another Depression like the one we had when I got here. There are safeguards now."

Sid saw the large crowd in front of the synagogue. "I think we'll walk on Pinehurst. How about it?"

They turned left at Washington Park across the street, in front of the 184th Street subway entrance, and walked by Hudson View Gardens. Sammy loved the English Tudor design and wished he could live there.

"There's a grocery store in the basement, you know," Sammy said.

"I didn't."

"Yeah, and Wes Westrum, Jim Hearn, and Al Worthington live there."

"Who?"

"The New York Giants," Sammy said.

"Oh. Well, you know, Sid Stone lives there, too," Sid said, referring to the "Milton Berle Show."

"Really? I thought they didn't let Jews in there."

"Sid Stone is Jewish. What was, was," Sid said.

"So we could live there? I always wanted to see what it looked like inside."

"It's old, older than our building. You don't want to live there," Sid said.

Sammy felt a twitch coming on so he bent his head down so his father wouldn't see.

"Dad?"

"Yes?"

"You know, we were supposed to go to shule tonight. What should I do about the rabbi?"

Sid thought for a moment. "Don't worry about it. We'll work it out. Mom will call. Don't you worry about it, okay?"

Still holding his hand, Sammy felt good again. It was like it always was. It was okay now. And they talked all the way home.

12

John Sticker was stirring his drink, looking at a Bemelmans mural behind the grand piano. The Carlyle was his favorite place to unwind. Stan Leopold came in and saw the bishop reading next to one of the small lamps that adorned each table.

"What's new?" he asked anxiously.

"'What's new?' How about, 'Hi, John. Nice to see you'?"

"I'm sorry. I'm all messed up over this thing. There's no excuse for that. I'm sorry. So how are you?"

"Now that's better. Thanks for asking. I'm doing fine. I already know how you're doing."

Stan sat and took off his coat.

"Thanks for meeting me here. I just love this place. You don't mind, do you?" John asked.

"John, of course not. I like it, too. It's one of the few watering holes that have character."

"Character," John said thoughtfully.

"What?" Stan asked.

"You have character, Stan. I've always thought that of you."

"Oh, shit. John, you're trying to tell me something I don't want to hear?"

Sticker laughed a little. "No, no, no, no, no."

"John, that chuckle is your political laugh. I don't think I like it very much. What's going on?"

"Can I order you something?"

"None of that. What gives?"

"Stan, have a drink. What are you gonna have? Some of that shitty ginger ale or a real drink? How about a Shirley Temple?"

"Fuck you," Stan said playfully and eyed the waiter.

"Yes, sir?"

"Let me have a bourbon and water, please."

"Atta boy."

"Thanks for your support, but enough of that. Thanks for meeting me. I'm getting a lot of pressure. People are very upset."

Sticker stirred his drink and took a sip. "It's serious, alright."

"What does that mean, really? You said you could handle this, that this wasn't your cup of tea or something like that. Didn't you say the pope wouldn't care for this? Peasants and all, you said."

Sticker shrugged and nodded but said nothing.

"For a gifted speaker, you seem reticent. I'm not hearing the Irish wit."

"Alright. Some people are viewing this as ridiculous, and some are viewing it as an opportunity. I thought this would be nothing, but it's turning into something because of Conway. He's going to milk this for all it's worth. I really don't blame him. I would do the same thing if I were in his shoes."

"What is it he actually wants?"

"To rebuild his church and be left alone."

"So?"

"Well, it's not as easy as all that. First it was in the pipeline to sell the property or do something else with it. I'm not sure which. Second, the church moves slowly."

"You said that. What are you saying? To them, I mean. What's your stand?"

"On Conway?"

"Yeah."

"I'm on the record discouraging the idea of making this a legitimate site, and most agree with me, especially when I point out that it's not a vision in the true sense. If it were a real vision, I promise you I would be on the other side. But it's not. I mean, I haven't seen it, but from what I know through a source, it is not something we could hang our hat on. On Conway? Well I'm not sure how I'm going to handle that."

"So when you say, 'hang your hat on,' your people have seen the door?"

"Let's just say I had someone check it out and he explained it to me."

"Bullshit. Who?"

"Stan, a crisp 100-dollar bill goes a long way."

"What if your position doesn't win the day? My people are driving me crazy, John. There's a mob in front of the synagogue praying, crying, and preaching. They're selling fuckin' hot dogs in front of the synagogue. Next Saturday is the bar mitzvah for this kid. We don't need John Cameron Swayze out there speaking about bar mitzvahs. You know the damn lumberyard that sold the doors to the synagogue is running a special! They're calling them 'Jesus Doors.' It's Goldberg's Lumber Yard, for Christ's sake. People buying these doors don't even have houses!"

"That's pretty funny," Sticker said, controlling his laughter.

"Oh great!" Leopold said.

"Okay, okay. I'll let you know something soon."

Stan shook his head.

"How's that drink?"

Stan took a deep breath and picked up his glass, then laughed. "You know, John, only a Goy asks a question like, 'How's your drink?' A Jew doesn't ask questions like that. Jews ask questions like 'How's business?' 'How's the family?' 'How's your life?' You ask how my fuckin' drink is. Jesus, a drink is a drink. We don't give a shit. We only drink ONE, for God's sake. It's a drink! But for you it's one of the major food groups. I should be asking you, 'How's YOUR drink?' It's almost like asking, 'Can you breathe?'"

Sticker laughed and grabbed Stan by the neck, kissing him on the forehead. "You know, Stan, you're my favorite—"

"SHHH! Don't say it," Stan cut him off. He stood and put on his coat.

"Stan, about those doors," Sticker inquired. "Do you think the Puerto Ricans are covering them with velvet?"

13

From 187th Street one could hear the noise emanating from the synagogue. Traffic heading downtown had lined up, horns blaring, people shouting. Sammy and his mother could hardly move and turned several times to get around the crowd. The scene looked like the television clips seen on the news. As they approached, Sammy could read the signs people were carrying. "Let us see the vision," read most of them, but there were others: "Religion a Mirage, Jesus a Reality," "The Torah speaks of Jesus," and '"No one can ignore Jesus forever." When they reached the area just in front of the synagogue, they stopped, not knowing exactly how to proceed. Sammy's mother had just gotten off the phone with the rabbi, and he was furious. She wanted to see him, but he refused. Now she looked at Sammy.

"Hold my hand," she said and pushed ahead. "Watch out!" she shouted. "Child!"

Sammy felt embarrassed. He hadn't held his mother's hand in years, yet he was proud of how she took command. The crowd relented, and Sammy and his mother made their way to the front doors. They passed the wooden stand that he'd seen being erected the night he followed his father to the bank, only now there was a sign above it: "Eat, Drink, and See Mary." "Mary" had a line through it, and "Jesus" had been written above it in a different script. Below that it read, "Hot dogs 65 cents, Pepsi 15 cents."

Finally they reached the front doors, where two policemen stood. A synagogue official recognized Mara and Sammy and ushered them inside. Once the metal doors shut behind them and the sound from the crowd muffled, Sammy was finally able to relax, until he thought of the rabbi.

"Mom," Sammy asked, "can we just practice at home? I know my haftorah."

"Don't worry, Sammy," his mother said. "It will be alright, but we have to talk to the rabbi." Sammy sat down near the rabbi's door while his mother opened it to let the rabbi's secretary know they were there. The door had a travel poster of Israel over it, which concealed the Jesus image.

Sammy's mother returned, sat down, and patted his knee.

"So where's this famous door?" she asked.

"Under the poster," Sammy said.

"I feel like I should peek," Mara said, smiling mischievously.

"No, mom!" Sammy nearly shouted.

"Okay, okay. Open your book. Practice."

"Mom, I know it."

"You can never practice too much."

Sammy opened his book and looked at his portion of the haftorah but didn't read a word. All he could think of was the rabbi. It seemed to Sammy as if he had known the rabbi all his life, yet Sammy had only arrived in Manhattan three years ago. This was only his second year of Hebrew school, but it felt to him as if he'd been going to the school forever. Every day he played in the schoolyard for an hour or two after school, then rushed toward the synagogue to go to Hebrew school. He never questioned it. He only let it be known how much he hated it.

He wondered how angry the rabbi really was. His relationship with Rabbi Gold had been unsatisfactory. He'd seen the rabbi at his angriest. The year before, while waiting for a bar mitzvah lesson, Barry and Sammy and a few other kids were lined up in the hallway in the old synagogue. The rabbi entered through the door in his black coat, and Sammy gulped some air and let out a belch as the rabbi walked by. The line of boys laughed in approval, until the rabbi stopped, turned, and looked.

"WHO DID THAT?!"

The boys shook their heads. "Not me," many of them said. But Rabbi Gold fixated on Sammy.

"You did it, didn't you?"

"No, Rabbi," Sammy pleaded.

"Yes, you did. Don't lie to me."

"No, I didn't, I swear," he said.

The rabbi inched closer to him and bent down so that they were face to face. Sammy stared at his stubble. He wasn't as clean-shaven as his father.

"Will you swear before the Torah?"

Sammy looked straight into the rabbi's eyes, squinting, trying to look honest. "Yes, Rabbi, I will."

"Come with me," the rabbi said and grabbed him by the top of his sleeve. Sammy followed awkwardly and looked back at the line of kids he was leaving. He smiled, but it was halfhearted. Sammy and the rabbi walked through the doors to the sanctuary. The creaking of the floors reminded him of services during the high holidays and how much fun he had during breaks from services playing ring-a-levio outside.

They came to a stop before the bimah, at the front of the sanctuary. Sammy was getting nervous. The rabbi wouldn't open the ark. Weren't there rules about opening the ark? One couldn't open it on a weekday night other than Friday, right? The rabbi let go of Sammy's shirt.

"Do you swear on the Torah that you did not belch?" he almost shouted, muting his voice in respect.

Without hesitation, Sammy said, "Yes. I swear, Rabbi." His face grew serious for effect.

The rabbi turned and opened the ark. Sammy's eyes widened as he examined the beautiful felt cover, which was embroidered with silver threading and the Lion of Judah designs with sterling silver rimonim and breastplate. He knew now the seriousness of the matter that he had gotten himself into. The rabbi had actually opened the ark.

"Look at the Torah, Mr. Levitt."

Sammy looked. He knew what was coming.

"Do you swear on this Torah that you did not belch?" Sammy stared at the Torah and wondered how heavy it was. Sometimes he would see older congregants have trouble holding it. He looked at the rabbi, who was fuming.

"Well?"

Sammy looked down at his shoes. "No, Rabbi."

The door to the rabbi's office opened, and Sammy snapped out of the memory. His mother rose and instructed Sammy to do the same.

The rabbi looked up from his desk as they walked in.

"Mrs. Levitt, how—"

"Rabbi," she interrupted. "I hardly know where to begin. I'm so sorry. I know you were angry and didn't want to see me, but we're here." The rabbi nodded and looked at Sammy but gave no expression. "I speak for my husband when I say we owe you an apology. Actually we owe you more than an apology. It's terrible outside, just terrible."

"Well...," the rabbi began.

But Mara continued, "My son Sammy is looking forward to his bar mitzvah and says he knows his haftorah."

"Yes, he was doing quite well..."

"And he is deeply sorry for all the trouble he caused. It was a lapse in judgment. He should have come to you first. Then this would have been a non-event."

Sammy was amazed at his mother. Here was the big difference between his mom and his dad, he thought. She was born here, not the old country. She knew how to talk to the rabbi. His father couldn't do it the same way. He would talk Yiddish and hope that would work. Sammy liked hearing older men talk in Yiddish. They seemed to know each other's past before any information was delivered. But here was mom showing her "Yankee-Doodle best."

"Rabbi, you have done a wonderful job. You don't get enough acknowledgment of that."

"Mrs. Levitt, please, enough. Thank you. Let me and Sammy work on his haftorah and you have some nachas when his day comes." Mara Levitt shook the rabbi's hand, kissed Sammy on the top of his head, and turned to leave.

"Mrs. Levitt, just a minute, please. While I have you… With this the first bar mitzvah in the new shule, we're going to start something new. In many synagogues now, parents are addressing their children on the bimah after the speech. I've had a lot of requests for this, and so we are going to initiate the practice at our congregation during Sammy's bar mitzvah. It's quite popular in Long Island. Mostly reformed, but conservative shules are doing it, too. So talk it over with your husband. It's a nice thing."

"Thank you, Rabbi."

"Sure. Now we'll get to work with your son. I guess we'll see you next time in shule."

"Goodbye. And come right home, Sammy," she said as she left. The rabbi walked around to his side of the desk, sat down, and fiddled mindlessly with some papers, thinking about what he wanted to say.

"Did you see what's going on outside?" he asked in a soft, nonthreatening way.

"I'm real sorry, Rabbi, but I just didn't think."

"No, I guess not."

Sammy relaxed a bit. He felt he could ask the rabbi a question.

"Rabbi, what's gonna happen?" he asked, his nose twitching.

"Sammy, I don't know. I haven't a clue, except sometimes when something is set in motion, it doesn't mean it can be stopped as easily as it was started."

"Can't the police stop it?"

"It's not a police matter. All the police can do is keep order, and that's why you see police outside. People have a right to stand on a sidewalk and carry signs. The hot dogs might be another matter. There's an expression, Sammy: 'You make your bed and you must lie in it.' This thing, this mishugas, has started, and it will have to play itself out. Not every story has a happy ending. We'll see." The rabbi thought to himself for a moment. "No, Sammy, you started something here, and I don't know how it's going to end. But it will…somehow. Anyway maybe you can be thinking about this when you write your speech." The rabbi looked at his desk. "What's your haftorah portion?"

"Isaiah 61:10–63:9."

"Hmm…that's right. Well, we'll see. You are working on your speech, yes?"

"In my head, Rabbi, but I am working on it, I promise."

The rabbi smiled disinterestedly at him.

Sammy had to push the door against the policemen outside to leave the synagogue. The crowd had grown. People coming from the subway station were backing up toward the escalator they were leaving. The noise was reminiscent of New Year's Eve at Times Square, but with a religious overtone. No one had any idea that the cause of this was snaking his way through toward home. Sammy thought about the content of his speech. He hadn't written a word, but tonight he would begin.

Dinner that night was different again. Only it was better. That is, it was like old times. Sammy heard his father put the key in the door and ran toward the sound. When Sid came in, Sammy ran up to him before he could take off his hat.

"What's this?" he asked, smiling.

"Nothing," Sammy said, and walked into the kitchen. Sid walked to the shelf in the foyer that held the home's three bottles of liquor. He opened the scotch, poured an ounce into a jigger, downed it, and smacked his lips. Then he walked into the kitchen and kissed Mara and looked over the stove. The phone was still off the hook.

"Ahhh!" he said, taking in the aroma. "So how did it go with the rabbi, or should I ask?"

"Okay, I think, considering."

"What do you mean, 'considering'?"

"I expected him to chew my head off, but he didn't. He was okay. So I mean considering that it was crazy outside. Jesus signs, people praying, the noise."

Manny walked into the kitchen.

"Hi, Dad."

"Hi, son."

Manny opened the Frigidaire and took out a beer.

"The rabbi talked to me about the bar mitzvah and said that in Long Island, naturally, the parents are giving speeches," Mara said.

"What are you talking about?" Sid asked incredulously.

"The parents give a short speech to the son. They're doing it in reform temples, Dad," Manny injected. "You and mom look at Sammy as if you're looking at Moses and say a few words. When I went to Coopersmith's little brother's bar mitzvah last month, his parents did it. They talk about how proud they are of their kid."

"Well, as a matter of fact," Sid injected, "at work today Uncle Sam came in, and I called out for sandwiches. We were talking about the bar mitzvah and he said the same thing. They are having themes for the bar mitzvahs now, like it's a story. Long Island, where else? If the boy likes to ski, then it's a skiing theme. Or if he wants to be a pilot, then it's airplanes. My theme in Poland was Jewish. A Jewish theme. You know, some people in the south eat shrimp at their bar mitzvahs? But Sam also said—wait till you hear this—he heard that some schmuck, not from Long Island but from Park Avenue no less, had a bar mitzvah at the Waldorf Astoria and served Japanese food. Do you know what they eat in Japan?" Mara stopped and looked, as did Sammy. "Raw fish! That's what they eat. Raw fish. And they're eating it here now. Mishugas!"

"So what's the theme for that one?" asked Manny. "Pearl Harbor?"

14

Again, the school day hadn't gone well. The joking had stopped, but Sammy didn't know what was worse—being made fun of, or being ignored entirely. Only Shelley spoke to him.

As Sammy approached his building, he decided not to go home. His parents were better about the mess, but he thought it best not to remind his mom while she was fixing dinner. So he hid his books in the bicycle room and headed toward the park.

Never had he been to the park as much as he had this past week. It was as if he'd always hung out there. Everything had changed—and so seemingly fast. Playing with Matt was another such change. He had nothing in common with Matt. Although they lived on the same side of the building, Sammy was never in Matt's apartment. He had no idea who his father was.

Yet here he was heading to the park again. Sammy enjoyed only one activity associated with the park, and it always occurred after dinner. Sid and Mara would walk through the main entrance and stroll to the flagpole and sit. Every evening the park was filled on that short path with German Jews who escaped the Third Reich or settled in Washington Heights after the war. Shelley's father made a living just getting reparations for people who had lost everything in Germany. They were Europeans, and they were continuing a European tradition. Sid would walk slowly with his hands clasped behind his back, and Sammy would listen as his mom and dad spoke of their lives and of the world. He loved it and felt that he would remember the stories spoken here the rest of his life. He hated to head back to the apartment, even for television.

Sammy arrived at the flagpole and looked out over the Hudson River. He thought about George Washington, and then about the battles fought here. Where were the old bullets in the ground? he wondered. He wished he had a metal detector. If he went into the wooded area of the park—the part that had not been landscaped, the part that was just as it was in 1775, where the same dirt and the same trees were—would he find the old ammunition? Anything could be there, he thought, down deep in the ground.

He turned from the flagpole and wandered down toward the Cloisters. He walked around the huge lawn that separated him from the building and stayed on the walkway. People were not allowed to walk on the grass. He wondered why it was okay to sled down Suicide Hill in the winter, but not to step on the fields anywhere else.

The door to the main entrance was open and he walked through. He wanted to see John Albert. Sammy proceeded slowly down the chilly hallways, entering some rooms, skipping others. Then he entered the arcade and garden court of the Cuxa Cloister and looked at the sky. Was this where Sara Churchill filmed her television show every Sunday? He'd never watched the show, but he would the next time he found it while changing channels. He left there and settled before a tapestry in the "Nine Heroes Tapestry Room." The word "Hebrew" caught his eye, and he began to read. He was staring at a fourteenth-century tapestry of Joshua, Judas Maccabeus, and David when he heard a familiar voice.

"That's King David with the harp," the voice said.

Sammy turned, already smiling. He wanted to hug John Albert.

"School over?" John Albert asked.

"Yeah." Sammy looked back at the tapestry. "That's Judah Maccabee, I bet."

John Albert leaned over for a closer look. "I think you're right. 'Judas Maccabeus' is what it says. Now that's the Latin."

"Judah Maccabee is all about Hanukah. He would pray to the Greek god Zeus or something like that," Sammy said.

"And so do you know how the eight days of Hanukah came about?"

"Yeah. Do you?"

"Sure. I had to learn the Maccabees also," said John Albert.

"Wow."

"How about coming with me? Are you hungry?"

"Yes," Sammy said, just then realizing that he was. John Albert pushed open a door, and Sammy found himself in a room from the twentieth century. The walls were plastered, and the ceiling had fluorescent lighting. It was a workstation that both surprised and disappointed him. Two monks were already seated and eating lunch. John Albert introduced them to Sammy and then took a container from the refrigerator. He opened the top and presented the contents to him.

"Here, take one."

"What is it?" Sammy asked, his nose twitching.

"Liverwurst or baloney and cheese. Take any one."

Sammy looked at the sandwiches. It looked like Wonder bread to him, and he just stared.

"It's okay. Go ahead. You can have one."

Sammy picked up the first one he saw and examined it more closely. The meat looked gray. A thin slice of American cheese sat right next to the gray meat. He peeled the corner of the bread back slowly and saw butter and mayonnaise stretching as he peeled. He brought the mayonnaise close so he could smell it. It smelled like mayonnaise, he thought…and butter. On meat, he thought. Gray meat.

"What's this one?" Sammy asked.

John Albert bent over and looked. "Let's see." Then he looked at his own sandwich. "Looks like liverwurst. Wanna trade? I got baloney."

"Is that okay?"

"Sure. Here," he said and handed Sammy his baloney sandwich.

Sammy slowly peeled back a corner again. Mayonnaise and butter stretched as they tried to hold on to the bread. Reddish meat, thinly sliced, with mayonnaise and butter and a piece of American cheese. Sammy's appetite dwindled.

"How's that?" John Albert asked.

"Great. Thanks." Sammy took his first bite near the corner, which had mostly bread but with a little baloney…and mayonnaise and butter…and cheese.

"How about a soda?" asked the monk. Yes! Sammy nearly shouted in gratitude and was handed a Pepsi with a bottle opener. He took small bites of the sandwich, following each with large gulps of Pepsi. Normally he wouldn't have been able to finish a twelve-ounce Pepsi, but he didn't think that would be an issue here.

"Two times in just a few days," John Albert stated.

"Huh?"

"Do you come here often? I've never seen you around before, I don't think."

Sammy's nose twitched. "I usually go to the schoolyard."

"The public school on Fort Wash?"

"Yeah, P.S. 187," Sammy said and took another small bite and another gulp of Pepsi. He wondered how much of the sandwich he could leave without insulting his new friend. He was more than halfway through.

"How's the sandwich, good?"

"Good," he said enthusiastically. "But I'm full. That's all I can eat. Thanks."

As they wandered toward the entrance, they passed through the Late Gothic Hall. Sammy stopped and looked up to the timbered ceiling. And then his attention was caught by the late medieval altarpieces that lined the front wall.

"What are these?" he asked.

"Retables, they're called, or altarpieces. They would rise high above the altars hundreds of years ago, and each told a story from the Bible. People were illiterate then, so this was one way of instructing them. These all came from different monasteries. Beautiful, aren't they?"

Sammy's eyes circled the room slowly. He sat down on one of the small wooden chairs lined in the center. John Albert joined him.

"I love the gold," Sammy said.

"It's Byzantine gold."

"It's beautiful."

"You're not Catholic, are you?"

"No," Sammy said.

"And you're not a Christian."

"No."

"Jewish?"

"How'd you know?"

"Just guessed," John Albert said, smiling. Sammy's nose twitched.

John Albert gestured for him to follow. They walked out onto the garden court of the Bonnefont Cloister, slowing as they rounded the well-manicured squares of plants. In the distance,

Sammy could see the George Washington Bridge, which reminded him of home.

"You're Sammy Levitt, aren't you?" John Albert asked gently.

Sammy thought for a second, afraid to answer, but then he looked at the young monk.

"Yes," he finally said, twitching his nose.

"You've got a lot on your plate."

"Plate?"

"Well, what I mean is, you've got a lot to handle according to what I've read in the papers. Your bar mitzvah and all."

"Oh, that. Yeah."

"Well, that's a big deal."

"Yeah, I know," Sammy said. The two of them stood side by side, looking out at the bridge.

"You know, I have an idea that might help you with that nose twitch you got going there," John Albert said.

Sammy turned toward him, embarrassed, not knowing how to respond.

"No, I mean it," John Albert told him. "I used to have something like that, but it was different. My eye twitched, and it drove me crazy. I was a little older than you, high school, about fifteen years old. I would blink my eye when I got nervous for some reason. It was all of a sudden, and I don't remember why it started. One day I got punched in the nose for winking at a guy."

Sammy laughed.

"So anyway, I developed, quite by accident, a way of camouflaging the blink. As soon as I felt the twitch coming on, I took my knuckle, just touched the side of my eye like this, and eventually it disappeared. Here..." John Albert took hold of Sammy's hand and raised it to Sammy's face. "What if you took your knuckle like this and just touched the side of your nose the next time you feel the urge? Do both sides if you have to. Just don't stick it in the hole."

They both laughed.

After that, they sat for a while, looking over the Hudson, not saying anything. Sammy was already using his knuckle. It seemed to help.

"Are you worried about the activity at the synagogue?"

"Yeah, I am."

"Well, things have a way of working themselves out," he said, placing his hand on top of Sammy's head. "You'll think of something."

As Sammy left the park, he found himself among the people exiting the subway. Sammy looked around for his father, but he wasn't in this mix. Then he heard a boom. As he approached his building, he noticed the number four bus stopped in front and the bus driver getting out and looking up. Sammy looked up as well and saw Matt Margolis on the roof. Dirt was falling from the roof of the bus, and the driver began a cursory inspection to find out what caused the loud crash. When he didn't succeed, he got back into the bus and drove off. A brown package hurtled down toward it, missing its rear end, and crashed to the smooth cobblestone street. Then Matt's head disappeared.

Sammy went up to the roof and found Matt by the front wall, packing dirt into small grocery bags.

"What the hell are you doing?" Sammy asked.

"This is great!" Matt answered.

"Did you hear that noise up here?"

"Shit, yeah. It was great."

Matt laughed, and so did Sammy but he was nervous. He wondered if anyone else had caught on. He wanted to join in, but he wasn't sure he could. It seemed too dangerous. He liked Matt because he seemed to do whatever he wanted to do, and even more because it appeared that Matt was one of the few who liked him.

"You want to throw one?"

"Nuh-uh!"

Matt looked over the wall, glancing both ways to see if another bus was coming. Then he turned around and put the bag down.

"Clear," he said as he sat down against the wall. Sammy sat down in front of him, crossed his legs, and watched as Matt began packing another bag. He thought about the logistics of this and wondered what kind of a person would go to all this trouble of carrying dirt from the backyard, up the elevator and to the roof. But Matt had no friends in the neighborhood, and Sammy never saw him with friends from his school. Sammy felt sad.

"I heard you're in trouble," Matt blurted out.

Sammy was surprised. Ever since the walk from the bank with his dad, he'd thought he wasn't in trouble anymore, that somehow the problem would go away on its own. But Matt was right, he thought. Even if he wasn't in trouble personally, how would the situation get better? He remembered Bombardment in the gym. Things weren't getting better.

"I mean, with all those people in front of the synagogue. What are you gonna do?" Matt asked.

Until that moment Sammy hadn't thought about what he was going to do.

"What can I do?" he asked earnestly.

"I don't know," Matt said, tying the bag with string, making it into a solid ball of dirt. Matt looked at Sammy, his eyes wide open with excitement.

"I know. Why don't you pull a 'Gandhi'?"

"A what?"

"A 'Gandhi.' Mahatmas Gandhi. You know who he is, right?"

"Yeah, of course. He freed India from the British."

"Right. And how did he do it?"

"How?"

"He stopped eating."

"And?"

"So, he was so popular that the British were afraid if he died, India would go ape-shit."

Sammy thought about it, rocking back and forth unconsciously as he pictured himself not eating. He saw himself at the dinner table just sitting there He wondered how that would work.

"So what happens if I stop eating?"

"They're not gonna let a kid die."

"And?"

"And, so you can do whatever you want. Ya see?"

"Yeah, I see," Sammy said, though he still wasn't sure he understood.

Matt got up and looked over the wall again.

Sammy looked at his watch.

"I'm freezing. I gotta go. See ya, Matt."

"If I should die so India can live, then so be it!" Matt shouted.

"Did Gandhi say that?" Sammy asked.

"I don't know. Sounds like he could have. See ya."

Sammy headed downstairs thinking about what Matt had said. A few minutes later, as he was entering his apartment, he noticed two policemen taking the elevator up. He wanted to warn Matt, but he knew he couldn't beat the elevator, and he knew that if he were caught with Matt, he would never be able to explain himself away. His parents didn't need any more trouble.

He thought that if he was going to stop eating, he would have to explain it to his parents.

When he entered his apartment, a man was sitting in the living room talking to his parents. Mara signaled for Sammy to come and sit.

"Sammy, this is Mr. Leopold. He's here to talk to us about the trouble at the shule. Say hello." Mr. Leopold stood up and extended his hand, and Sammy shook it.

"Sit, sit," Mr. Leopold said.

"You were saying before Sammy came in, about the phone?" Mr. Leopold asked.

"We don't answer it. We just call out. And we leave the phone off the hook. Just today I had a religious man knock. I can't even open the door without getting nervous," Mara said.

Sammy hadn't thought about what happened at the house when he wasn't there. He looked at the small glass cigarette lighter on the coffee table and wanted to pick it up to examine it. He loved that lighter with the tiny seahorse in it. Sammy wasn't sure if seahorses were real. They looked too perfect to be real—just like a horse but not a horse. And they moved like cartoon characters.

"Listen, it's not easy. What can I tell you? But we'll get through it. Right, Sammy?" Sid said.

Sammy looked down. Mara stroked his head.

"Well, thank you for the coffee and the cake. Very good, Mrs. Levitt," Mr. Leopold said as he rose. Sammy stood up, then sat as Mara walked Mr. Leopold to the door. Sammy could hear them speaking in the hall with the door open. They seemed to be whispering. The situation must be very serious, Sammy thought.

Later, Sammy went into his room and rested his head on a pillow. He stared at the model airplanes hanging from his ceiling. The light magnified the dust building up on the wings of the P-47

Thunderbolt that was positioned above and closing in behind the Japanese Zero. Every time Sammy saw the dust building up on those wings, he imagined blowing it off. He liked to think about these planes and the others hanging from the ceiling, but he couldn't this night. All he could think about was the door at the shule, and the rabbi and the school, and now Mr. Leopold. He felt himself getting angry at the priest.

He heard Manny and Sid come in and his mother calling for dinner. When he didn't respond, she came to his room and sat down on his bed. Before she could say anything, Sammy spoke.

"I'm not hungry, Mom. I have an upset stomach."

Mara touched his forehead.

"You don't have a fever. Maybe I'll make you tea and toast later if you don't eat."

"Thanks, Mom," Sammy said, feeling good about the decision he had made not to eat.

15

School was becoming routine again, only it was a different routine. The larger the crowd grew in front of the synagogue, the farther the kids shied away from Sammy. Shelley still spoke to him and invited him over to his house after school. But Sammy found himself drawn to kids who didn't do well in school, like him, who lived on the perimeter of the socially acceptable. They weren't as judgmental, he felt.

He'd known Marvin since moving to Washington Heights, but he'd hardly ever spoken to him given how stupid Marvin was considered to be, having been left back a grade. After the events at the synagogue, Sammy made an effort to get to know him, and soon Marvin invited Sammy home to play. He lived close to 181st Street in one of the older apartment buildings. Marvin brought out his Monopoly game, but before too long Sammy became anxious and said he had to go. The troubles at the synagogue were trumping everything.

Sammy felt fearful as he walked up the short hill toward the synagogue. The crowd outside had billowed into the street, creating a traffic jam. He turned around and decided to go by way of Cabrini Boulevard. He wouldn't be noticed there. As he walked past Hudson View Gardens, he thought of his time with Marvin. Marvin hadn't done anything wrong, but Sammy didn't enjoy himself, and he couldn't figure why. Marvin wanted to play, and Sammy was grateful someone other than Shelley wanted to see him. But it wasn't like going over to Shelley's house or even playing with Matt. And then he thought of his mother and pictured the phone off the hook.

He wondered about his father, too. Was he getting more phone calls? He couldn't take his phone off the hook. What was it like for him at work?

As he came closer to home, Matt's idea of Gandhi grew on him more and more. He felt a new determination.

"How are you feeling, Sammy?" his mother shouted as he entered the apartment and passed the kitchen.

"Fine."

"Did you eat your sandwich?"

"Yes," he lied. Then he went over to the encyclopedia that rested on the few shelves of books in the foyer and opened it to "Mahatmas Gandhi." With a paper and pencil, he copied out ten of the man's sayings and placed them on his nightstand. He examined the first one and began the process of memorizing them.

Later he heard his father enter the apartment and pictured him hanging his coat, going to the small cabinet in the foyer, taking out a bottle of scotch, and pouring himself a shot—one gulp and a smack of the lips—every night, as if it were a prescription. Sammy felt a twitch coming on and quickly knuckled his nose. For a moment he felt great. At least one thing was working. Something was working. His stomach growled, and he wanted desperately to have one of his mother's "forshpeis," one of Sammy's favorite words in Yiddish, an appetizer. But he decided that tonight they would learn of his decision to fast.

Manny came home from downtown, and Mara called for Sammy to come to dinner. He stayed in his room, on his bed with his hands behind his head. Mara called again, and then he heard her tell Manny to get him.

"Hey, putz...dinner!" Manny called when he came to the door. When Sammy's feet didn't move, Manny entered the room and faced his little brother.

"Hey, douchebag, dinner is ready."

Sammy stifled a laugh but said nothing, still resting the back of his head on his hands, looking at his airplanes.

"Hey, do I look invisible?" Manny asked, annoyed.

Sammy said nothing, eyes staring at the ceiling.

"Dinner, Sammy. Come on!"

Sammy still didn't move, still didn't look at Manny.

"Hey, what's wrong?"

Sammy lowered his eyes and stared into his brother's.

"I am prepared to die, but there is no cause for which I am prepared to kill," Sammy said.

"WHAT?"

Sammy didn't reply.

"What the hell was that?"

"Gandhi," Sammy said, and stared back at the airplanes.

"What the hell are you talking about?"

Sammy continued to stare. Manny left the room.

"So where's Sammy?" Sid asked.

"I think Sammy needs to see you. I don't know," Manny said, as he pulled a beer from the Frigidaire.

Sid went into the boy's room, followed by Mara. They saw Sammy resting on his back, staring at the ceiling.

"What's this?" Sid said, concerned. Mara stared at him, drying her hands on a towel.

"There is more to life than simply increasing its speed," Sammy said.

Sid, befuddled, turned to Mara.

"Talk to him," he said.

Mara sat on the bed. "What's going on, son?" she said, feeling his forehead.

"I'm not eating," he said, letting it out.

"Why not?" Sid almost yelled.

"I'm on a hunger strike, like Mahatmas Gandhi."

"Why?" Sid said.

"Because if I should die so India can live, then so be it."

"INDIA! What the hell are you talking about?" Sid yelled.

Manny came back into the room.

"Mom, Dad. Let me talk to him alone," Manny said as he ushered his parents away. Manny sat down on the bed next to his brother.

"Alright, little fella. What's this all about? You're gonna drive everybody nuts."

"That's my plan."

"What plan?"

"To stop the stuff at the shule. The phone calls."

"Okay. So how can you stop that by not eating? Explain that to me, why don't you?"

"They won't let me die."

Manny looked at him and thought about what he said. Then he pursed his lips and nodded, indicating some agreement.

"I get it. Do what Gandhi did, right?"

"Right."

"Stupid idea. All you are gonna do is drive Mom and Dad crazy, and you won't stop shit."

Sammy folded his arms and looked to the ceiling.

"Live as if you were to die tomorrow," Sammy said.

"Jesus H. Christ," Manny groaned, leaving the room.

16

The next day when Sammy arrived home from school, he was surprised to see Rabbi Gold sitting in the living room. Sitting opposite him was his mother, bent over with her head in her hands. She looked to Sammy and opened her arms for him to come to her. He came to her slowly, though not hesitantly, as he knew it would hurt her if he held back. She grabbed him and held him close, reached up and felt his scalp.

"Hello Sammy," the rabbi said.

"Hello, Rabbi."

"The rabbi wants to talk to you. I need to get dinner ready."

"Sit, Sammy," the rabbi said. "Do you think you're ready?"

"I'm ready, Rabbi."

"What about your speech?"

"I'm ready, I think."

"Good. Good. That's good," the rabbi said uncomfortably. "Your mother says that you're not eating, that you're trying to put a stop to all this mishugas by starving yourself. This is very dangerous, Sammy. You can get sick, or worse, God forbid."

Sammy could smell the food cooking. He wanted to eat. His stomach was no longer growling, and when he drank water, it helped but only for a while.

"I know," he said, with his head down.

"So why don't we stop this? This vision business will pass. I don't know how, but sooner or later there will be an end to this. I admire you for what you're trying to do. I'm just afraid that if you are hurt in the process, nobody wins. Do you see?"

"Yes, Rabbi."

"Good. Then you'll have dinner tonight?"

"We must become the change we want to see in the world," Sammy said.

The rabbi stared at him, his mouth open.

17

Sammy walked to school the next morning in a daze. Once again he hadn't eaten breakfast, but he'd given into his mother and taken two pieces of buttered toast wrapped in a paper towel, which he'd placed in his jacket pocket. He met Shelley as he was leaving his apartment building, and listened to him as they walked to school. He looked at the sidewalk as Shelley talked. Each crack in the concrete appeared as a divide to breach. Could he make it? Did he have to jump each line that he saw? The lines became valleys, and Shelley's voice became louder. He looked down and wondered why Shelley was shouting, wondered why Shelley didn't hear him answer his questions. He was answering them, wasn't he?

When they arrived at school, each went to his first class. Sammy grabbed hold of the green handrail as he climbed the stairs. The railing was cold, he thought. Ice cold. He began to slow as he climbed. He stopped when he got almost to the top. The last step looked higher. He placed his books on the landing and pressed his hands on one knee to push his body up the rest of the way. Then he picked up his books again and headed for class.

His class was language arts. Miss Devaney was talking about a dangling participle, and Sammy felt like one. The room was spinning. He raised his hand, but didn't know why. Then he began to laugh. All heads turned toward him. They appeared to be yelling at him, and he wondered why Miss Devaney didn't stop them. Then the room went white—completely white—and quiet. The spinning stopped. Sammy's eyes were wide open, and the back of his head felt cold. He was lying on the floor, staring into the white ceiling. Faces from all sides peered into him. Sammy saw them as if they were a kaleidoscope.

P.S. 187 hadn't seen this much excitement since a visit by real Brooklyn Indians in full headdress. The ambulance arrived around noon after Sammy passed out and took him to Jewish Memorial Hospital on Broadway. Soon Mara arrived at the hospital, and behind her, television crews. When Sid and Manny arrived, they had to push through a mob of news reporters and other people. As they passed through, they could hear one reporter talking through his microphone.

"Young Sammy Levitt," he began as Sid and Manny passed, "the boy who saw the vision of Jesus Christ at a synagogue in Washington Heights, was brought to Jewish Memorial in an incoherent state. Witnesses say that he was speaking in tongues. But that hasn't been confirmed."

Stan Leopold pushed through the crowd, looking for Sammy's parents. Soon Bishop Sticker was let through by the police, followed by Rabbi Gold. Finally they were all gathered in the waiting room, anxiously awaiting news.

"It's crazy out there," Sticker said.

"What have I been telling you?" Stan replied.

Mara was sitting with Sid, holding his hand and rocking. She caught Stan's eye and he went over to her.

"Is that the priest?" she asked.

"Yes. I mean, no, no. He's a priest, but not the priest from St. Mary's. No, no. He's actually not a priest. He's a bishop. John Sticker, a good friend, and someone who is trying to help us," Stan said.

He introduced Sticker to the Levitts. Rabbi Gold came over and Sid introduced him to Stan and Sticker.

Sticker pulled Stan aside.

"How is he?" Sticker asked.

"I don't know anything. I don't think anyone does," Stan said. They stood quietly for a moment, taking in the scene. The noise was getting louder outside, and police were trying to push the crowd away from the hospital. Mara began to cry and Rabbi Gold tried to console her. Stan and Sticker moved over to the side.

"This is serious. This kid can't die," Sticker said.

"John, if this kid dies, some schmuck will try to make him a saint. And if that happens, I can promise you one thing."

"What's that?"

"I'll blow your fuckin' brains out."

Sticker smiled, stifling a laugh, and placed his arm on Stan's shoulder.

"The boy won't die," Sticker said, looking around. "I'll take care of this."

Sticker walked over to the Levitts and wished them encouragement before leaving.

The next morning brought good news to the Levitt family. Sammy had responded well to treatment, and he began the day with a real breakfast. He would be able to leave very soon. All he was suffering from was exhaustion and dehydration. Later Manny gathered Sammy's old clothes and wheeled him out through a fist of reporters. Gabe Pressman was the first to reach Sammy.

"Sammy, tell us, how does it feel to be the center of all this attention?" he asked.

Manny stepped between Pressman and Sammy, placed his hand over Sammy's mouth, and looked at the reporter.

"Never miss a good chance to shut up!" Manny said.

"Gandhi?"

"No. Will Rogers."

18

Manny stood behind Sammy, adjusting his tie before the bedroom mirror.

"Are you ready, big boy?" Manny asked.

Sammy felt a twitch coming on and gently touched each side of his nostril. Then he smiled. Manny hadn't noticed.

Manny stepped back and approved of his work with Sammy's tie.

"There you go. How's your speech? Are you ready? You should have let me help you."

"I got it, Manny. I'm ready."

"Well, let me give you some tips, okay?"

"Okay."

"Alright. Be attentive to how quickly you speak. You don't want to race through this thing, or no one will understand you. Speak slowly, and after a few sentences, stop and look to the left side of the congregation and then to the right. Make eye contact with the audience. It will help you to relax. Okay? Look at me once in a while. I will give you a signal if I have to."

"Okay."

"Did you thank Mom and Dad in your speech?"

"The rabbi gave me an outline of things to include."

"Did you thank me, the jewel in the crown?"

"Yeah," Sammy said, laughing.

It was a cool, brisk morning. The sky was cloudless as they walked south on Fort Washington Avenue towards the Fort Washington Jewish Center. Milling about in front of the synagogue were other Levitts and friends of the family. What was missing were the throngs of people demanding entrance. So, too, was the hot dog stand, as everyone was now behind barricades a few blocks south. Just a solitary policeman was in attendance to ensure order. Sammy looked around for the crowd and saw another policeman down the block. Then he looked at the park and saw another and another. Farther down, by 181st Street, he saw still another barrier, which held back a large group of people. But right here it was like it used to be, and he felt good about that. He saw Mr. Richter, the old man who ran the newsstand. He was there, just like always. He looked at him and smiled. Richter did not smile back. He never smiled. Sammy could not recall that he ever spoke, except to give out numbers: "fifty cents," "seventy-five cents."

Sammy entered the synagogue, his face tattooed with red lipstick from his aunts. He was smiling and knuckle-nosing and loving every minute. He reached into the side pocket of his blue suit and touched his speech. In his head he was humming the first few bars of his haftorah portion.

When he passed the rabbi's office, he noticed the door was gone, and leaning against the wall next to the opening was a brand new door, unpainted and possessing no discernible images. He wondered where the old door was. The rabbi's assistant was standing in the doorway and smiled at him.

After entering the sanctuary, the rabbi saw him and motioned him forward and whispered in his ear. Sammy walked to the back of the bimah and sat on a chair facing the congregation. He went row by row, recognizing each of his cousins, his aunts and uncles, returning their smiles as they cautiously waved to him. Sid and Mara sat next to Manny and kept turning as people whispered and tapped their shoulders. They had already had the experience five years earlier with Sammy's older brother, but it never got old.

Sammy remembered his father describing his own bar mitzvah in the old country, how his grandfather took Sid to shule on a Thursday morning with a bottle of Slivovitz. After services everyone had a schnapps, and Sid was given a piece of chocolate as a present. There was no family in attendance—not even his mother was at the shule. But this was America, and it was 1954. Things had changed.

The rabbi walked casually over to the window overlooking the front of the building. He stood for a moment and looked out at the small park across the street. A few older men were playing chess on the concrete tables. He thought he recognized a few as congregants.

There was no shouting now. Only splinters remained of the hot dog stand. For a change, he thought, praying would be in the building, not on Fort Washington Avenue. It was normal again, but he knew it was temporary.

He turned and saw Sammy. He watched as Sammy acknowledged his family coming into the sanctuary. As he watched, he marveled at how an innocent chance gesture begun by a thirteen-year-old in his synagogue might end in a way so incalculable that his own life as a rabbi may have changed forever. Perhaps this is the new normal. And he wondered with a sadness, and a realization, that this might be his new life, and he wondered if he could continue.

Two blocks away Stan Leopold emerged from the 181st Street subway station and weaved his way through the crowd, corralled by sawhorses and policemen. He showed his I.D. to a cop and headed toward the synagogue. As he crossed the street, he passed by St. Mary's and saw two men on the roof working on the slate tiles. Below were other men carrying a piece of plywood. He headed north, recounting his recent phone call from the bishop. It had all been taken care of, he was told. The door was going to a place for safekeeping, and the story would be that it was the wish of Rome that the door be placed where it could be properly admired by Christians from around the world. Stan smiled as he recalled John Sticker's most persuasive remark to the leadership. What if the Jews made the door into 2,000 pencils? Now that's an idea, he thought, as he walked into the synagogue and took a seat in the back of the sanctuary.

The service moved along as usual. Sammy knew what his parts would be. Being a bar mitzvah, he would partake in the service as an adult, reading from the Torah as his ancestors had for over 5,000 years. He was surprised at his nervousness. He had been doing just fine until he heard the rabbi call Sammy's Uncle Max for an aliyah. Sammy stood by the rabbi as his uncle came up, kissed him on the cheek, and read. Then Uncle Dave and Uncle Irving did the same. When Sammy's turn to read arrived, he looked at the Torah and it startled him. He stared at the vellum and the hand-painted words in Hebrew. He had never been this close to an open Torah. The rabbi gave him the sterling-silver pointer and directed him to the right space. Sammy froze. There were no dots or dashes below the letters to help him pronounce the words. He looked at the rabbi, who touched his shoulder.

"Don't worry," he said. "You know this. You'll recognize the words as you go along. You can do this, Sammy." He hummed the first few bars, signaling Sammy to begin. And he did, pausing once to look at his parents for approval.

When he concluded, the rabbi shook his hand, followed by the cantor.

Later, after the closing of the ark, the rabbi stood behind the bimah. He took out a few sheets of folded paper and laid his speech down on the lectern. It was a simple speech, maybe one he picked out of a book of sermons. It wasn't topical, and there were no references that would have given notice that it was recently written or timely. It was rather a generic speech about helping those in need. He was popular for his intellect. He loved history and tied his sermons to it. One didn't always come away feeling good, but one almost always came away feeling like one had learned something. This sermon, however, gave one the feeling that he had a bus to catch. The door. That damned door was on his mind. And the reason, the cause, sat behind him trying to become a man in the eyes of God. A thirteen-year-old boy.

The rabbi turned, motioned Sammy to the front, and whispered in his ear. It was time for his speech. The rabbi turned and sat down at the rear.

Sammy looked at his parents and saw Manny making a gesture with his hands to keep it slow, and he remembered.

"I spoke with Rabbi Gold a few days ago concerning my speech and asked him if I could do something different today. Instead of tying my speech to my Torah portion, I want to talk about something that happened, something that you all know about. Last Friday night I talked with my dad while we walked back from the bank. I wish I had spoken to him earlier." Sammy stopped for a moment. "I need to say this. I didn't see a vision, as the newspapers said. A vision is like a live appearance or something. I just saw what looked like…" He turned to the rabbi, walked over to him, whispered something, and returned to the podium. "I just saw a design, and I thought it looked like something. It wasn't a vision. Well, you all know the rest. I asked my dad what was going to happen to the Fort Washington Jewish Center. He said it would be resolved. Rabbi Gold also told me it would be resolved, but I'm not so sure. I think I really started something, and I want to apologize to Rabbi Gold, to my parents, and to all of you. I think the only Torah portion I could relate this to is one that says, 'Look before you leap,' if that existed. I learned a big lesson from all of this, and that is, that there is not always a happy ending. The rabbi told me that. 'Sometimes,' he said, 'we can't make things as they were, and a new reality sets in, and we have to learn to live with that.' But I hope it can go back to the way it was. Especially for the rabbi."

Rabbi Gold came to Sammy and shook his hand, and motioned to Sid and Mara. He waited a moment and motioned them again.

Manny leaned. "Mom, Dad, here is where you talk to Sammy. You know, the talk."

Mara turned to Sid.

"Sid, we talked about this. Parents talk to the children," she said anxiously.

Sid shrugged.

"Manny, we're not prepared. You talk. You're better at this than we are," Mara said urgently.

"C'mon, Mom, you can do this. You'd be better at this than Dad."

"It'll be nice if you do it. You're young. You're his brother. He looks up to you. Go, go," she said.

Manny got up, walked over to the rabbi, and whispered in his ear. The rabbi nodded and sat down. Then Manny walked over to Sammy and placed his hands on his shoulders and looked at him directly in the eyes.

"Sammy, I've known you all your life, all your thirteen wonderful years. I know everything about you. Your likes, your dislikes, your favorite baseball player, your favorite ice cream." Manny looked out at the congregation trying to find the right words. He looked at his parents, sitting, almost looking cute to him now. He noticed tears from his mother's eyes. He turned back to Sammy.

Sammy loved Manny. Manny made him laugh. Manny played with him, even though he was so much older—well, when he wasn't busy, he did. Sammy wondered what he was going to say that his mom and dad couldn't.

"Sammy," Manny said and looked at the congregation again, then to Sammy, and then to the rabbi. "Sammy, the last few weeks have been very trying. On top of schoolwork you had to learn your haftorah portion, which you handled very well today. But then there was all the..." Manny hesitated, not knowing exactly how to say it. "But then, here was the issue of the troubles outside, which occurred very innocently. You had a lot to deal with, and your speech to that issue was appropriate." Sammy smiled as the words became stronger. "So, Sammy," Manny said, turning to his parents and the congregation, now smiling broadly, the words coming easily now. "So, Sammy," he repeated more forcefully, "I can say this from the bottom of my heart, and with all honesty, that to the best of my knowledge, you are not now, nor have you ever been, a member of the Communist Party."

Who Cries for Aaron?

He watched the woman go into the restaurant and followed her inside. The restaurant once served as a stable for Roman soldiers. Now it was Mario's, not unknown to tourists even here, so far from Florence. Across the front window pane was a large white curtain embroidered with intricate thread designs, engaging each other as in a dance. It was heavy enough that Danny couldn't see through it, and he thought the restaurant to be elegant.

The front door was dressed with large, swirling medallions of brass protecting clouded carved glass. When Danny touched the door to go in, he left his fingerprints and remembered the large brass entrance doors to his apartment building in New York when he was a child. He remembered Eddie, the janitor, polishing the doors to a clear field of gold reflecting the backs of tenants as they went off to work each morning. And he remembered coming home from school and pushing through the same doors and never being able to see his reflection in the brass. One smudge to Danny was like a mistake—100 smudges, disrespect.

Inside the restaurant he was greeted by an old man who smiled officiously and gestured for his coat. Danny hesitated, realizing that he would have to tip the man, and he became momentarily afraid, unsure of the expense, as if the tip might require a sum greater than the cost of the meal. But he surrendered the garment, feeling a bit uneasy because it was a windbreaker and not a dress coat. He walked into the dining area, past a ceremony of antipasto on a side table: cold, thin asparagus marinated in herbs and spices, sliced meats, roasted red peppers and vegetables he didn't recognize, squid and whole fresh fish that looked as though they were swimming on beds of ice. It was Friday.

Danny was shown to a table across from the woman he had watched earlier in the day. He hoped that he wouldn't be noticed. He saw her remove her kerchief, arch her neck, and shake out her hair. She was prettier here, he thought, and more relaxed. As she turned to examine the surroundings, she looked his way and he froze. He was sure she recognized him from the park and would know that he had followed her. Danny looked down and pretended to read his menu, realizing there wasn't a word of English on the card. When he looked up, she was ordering, but with much difficulty. He was right in his assumption: she wasn't Italian.

At another table near him a young man sat reading a newspaper. A small dog sat by his feet like a stuffed toy. The dog's eyes were fixed on another dog three tables away. The dogs seemed perfectly at ease.

The waiter rolled a tray before the man's table, brandishing a neatly formed mound of raw, finely chopped beef resting in a shallow pool of olive oil. The man put down his paper, examined the beef, and nodding his approval to the waiter, returned to his paper. The waiter approached his work like an artist. He began by seizing a tablespoon and making a depression on top of the beef. Then he broke an egg and separated it, depositing the yolk in the crater, pressing it into the meat, and folding it in with great exaggeration like a violinist. He folded the egg with the olive oil until what remained was another neatly formed mound. The man engaged in his newspaper was not watching the performance, and it annoyed Danny. Around the edge of the plate were small mounds of pepper, salt, diced onion, mustard, and minced garlic, along with a pool of lemon juice. The waiter's spoon darted out from the center of the plate to snatch ingredients like a painter spearing his oils from a pallet, until all the ingredients were combined, and an order of steak tartare was presented. Danny wondered if he could find what he had just seen on the menu and whether he could get the waiter to understand him. But he wanted it cooked, medium. They wouldn't respect well-done here, he thought.

When a waiter finally came, Danny ordered spaghetti, a salad, and a glass of wine. He liked to order wine. It made him feel older than his twenty-two years.

The woman was eating when the waiter brought his small carafe of wine. He liked the way she put down her utensils after each bite. He liked the way she looked up, the way her lips closed and moved slowly and deliberately as if she were testing something. After his roommate in college had ridiculed him for his eating habits, he vowed to eat always with his mouth closed.

He stared at the woman as he sipped his wine and reflected on the events of the day. He thought about the first time he'd seen her. Earlier that day he'd been in a bus heading for Foto Pass, about five miles away, in a mountainous region in northern Italy, just south of the Austrian border. He remembered looking at the countryside but not really seeing it. He had been thinking of his grandfather, remembering how his grandfather could become so mired in the seat of his couch that it appeared to be molded to him. Danny loved that couch because he, too, could make a hole and try to hide in it, and indeed, when small, he had to strain to get out, a struggle that delighted his grandfather.

Danny enjoyed his grandfather because of the stories. To him they were as exciting as any pirate's tale he had read, and yet they were merely sketches of his family in Austria before the war. Mostly he yearned for stories about his brother, Aaron.

"Your brother was very brave, Danny," the old man said, waving his finger slowly. "Brave in a time when we Jews were afraid." His grandfather was fat, with bold brown eyes and a walrus mustache that gave him the demeanor of a White Russian in exile. A man of authority. Only he was not a White Russian. He was Austrian. A tired old Austrian Jew whose only pleasure now was pinochle, his grandson, and long walks in the park near his apartment in uptown Manhattan.

He had always spoken slowly and easily to Danny, like an indulgent tutor, and because of this, Danny thought he was wise. The wise are always old and cautious—and slow, Danny believed.

"Honor the memory of your brother," his grandfather had said. "Be filled with his courage."

The stories of his brother had inspired Danny, but they distressed his parents.

Danny wondered why his parents never discussed his brother as he was growing up, and why they discouraged his grandfather from doing so. What the young boy could not comprehend was the kind of insanity that rakes the mind of its spirit, the disease that comes from the loss of a child. That even grew in Danny, for he wouldn't talk of his brother to his friends. He shielded his brother's death like he would a vicious scar on his back, never letting down his guard, as if to say to the world, "I will not take off my shirt."

It was his secret. Only what he did not realize was that there are no secrets, and children treat a confidence like a contest, so everyone who knew Danny also knew his burden. While his friends clipped pictures of baseball players from sports magazines and plastered them on their walls, Danny had his private hero and worshipped him silently.

Danny had watched the scenery numbly and thought of his grandfather, and then he heard the bus driver's announcement for Foto Pass. He left the bus and stood beneath a brilliant Italian sun, with only a golf cap to shade his eyes. He hesitated and then walked down a bordered gravel path toward the main entrance to the cemetery. He felt uneasy. Nothing felt the way he had imagined. This was too quick, he thought. He had pictured this moment for years, had practiced it with his grandfather in mind, the two of them walking together slowly, silently to uncover a hidden and lonely tombstone.

As he looked over the valley that gave way to the flatlands before Florence, he began to rethink his picture, and then he realized why he felt so uneasy. He had envisioned a cemetery like the ones pictured in old books around the house. Tall, unkempt grass strangling rusty ironwork, fencing in tombstones, which leaned from side to side as if the graves themselves were weary, the stones barely legible, begging to be recognized and revered for at least one more generation. "There is no sunlight in a German sky," his grandfather had said once. Danny hadn't known what his grandfather meant, but he had always pictured Aaron in a field of gray.

This was different. Short, cropped grass cushioned his feet like a showroom carpet. Italian gardeners dressed in colorful baggy pants with heavy twisted ropes around the waist were trimming the tall hedge rows that guarded the cemetery. A granite wall with mortar still white from a recent painting traced the hedges around the park. It was all clean and orderly. Each tombstone lay flat like flagstones in a patio. Danny began to walk the rows, eager to find Aaron's grave. German war dead in Italy, all of them. How strange to be buried in the wrong place, he thought.

He paced the rows quickly, looking, but not closely, his eyes jumping ahead to other rows and other stones. He wanted the moment to be memorable, like a discovery. It felt good to have come, to have accomplished what he promised for so long. He regretted only that his grandfather wasn't alive. If he were, he thought, he wouldn't feel so lonely.

Behind him, and towering at the crest of the hill, a monument jutted toward the valley like a gun turret. Concrete, sharp-cornered, and defiant, it lured Danny like an occult message. It stood about twelve feet tall and, though three-sided, offered one narrow entrance, which could be reached at the rear. Through the opening Danny could a see a few lit candles. The walls were two feet thick, and there was less room than the outside appearance indicated. Danny's eyes had to adjust from the sunlight as he entered. The light inside was subdued, allowing the candles to create a mood of reverence. Fresh wreaths lined the coarse gray walls, mirroring the last war. Red, green, yellow, and blue flowers commemorated a Panzer division, and another, artillery. There were others. Beyond the candles, a swastika of fresh red, black, and white flowers stood in direct view of the visitor. It was menacing to Danny, yet beautiful, and he felt like an archeologist uncovering a species long believed to be extinct.

He stood in awe beneath the evil he saw celebrated, feeling mocked, deceived, and afraid. It never ends, he thought. Like a virus it explodes periodically, then recedes quietly to fester. The fear in Danny became anger, and he wanted to strike with his own words across the walls, in German. But he knew very little German, and the thought of writing the words in Yiddish so that they might be understood made him feel impotent. The cries in the gas chambers were in Yiddish.

Danny exited the monument exhausted. He sat on the grass beside the memorial and looked beyond the park to the valley. Outside were Italy and the present, inside the horrors of the past. He sat wondering why he felt that a curse from a German, or a Christian, was more valid than one from himself. Why did he feel it absurd for him, a Jew, to curse a Nazi, and why did he place a Christian in the same camp as the enemy? Was it because his image of a Christian was that of a colossus, or was it that his own image was not that of David, the boy who slew Goliath, but more of a fearful east European Jew garbed in a black overcoat running from the hooves of a charging Cossack?

He was still sitting on the grass when he noticed a woman with heaving breasts spread a blanket beside a grave. She was a big woman with a pleasant round face. A tight leather belt pulled in her waist. Danny imagined her taking off the belt at night and billowing out to a bulbous shape. She was joined shortly by her husband, a robust man in his fifties with a flushed face and wearing a green alpine hat with a brown feather that seemed to befit him. They opened a wooden basket and decorated the blanket with fruit, cheese, and wursts. While the husband struggled with a bottle of wine, the woman called her little boy, who was running up and down the rows imitating an airplane. It seemed to Danny that she was annoyed.

Later, as the woman spread dark mustard over black bread, she looked up and saw Danny. She was five or six rows down the hill, and she had to shield her eyes from the sun to look in his direction. She smiled, and Danny waved to her and heard himself give out a shallow "hello" that sounded as though it came from a toy doll. He cleared his throat and looked around uncomfortably. The woman turned to her husband, who had started eating, and said something. He nodded in agreement and she turned to Danny and motioned for him to join them.

The woman was full with middle age. Her arms were puffed like small bedrolls, and her face, except for an unattractive birthmark, was clear and inviting. Danny felt warm next to these strangers. They tried to converse in German, but it was soon clear that Danny spoke very little, and when they tried English, that proved futile.

"Nicht gut, nicht gut," the man said with an exaggerated frown as he pointed to the graves in a sweeping motion.

"Yah, nicht gut," Danny agreed as he swallowed a lump of moist bread.

"American?"

"Yes, ya, ya."

The man smiled, then touched Danny's shirt, indicating how he came to that conclusion. Danny pointed to the stone nearest to them and told them he was sorry.

"Ya, ya, nicht gut." And with a wave of his hand as if to dismiss the subject, the man indicated that it was a long time ago.

By pointing to Danny and then to the memorial, the woman asked why he was there. Danny thought for a moment, and then he moved his arms in a semicircle as if he were driving a car. He opened his eyes wide, making a dramatic gesture at the site of the cemetery as he drove by. The couple understood; he was on vacation. It was their vacation, too. He learned that many Germans came here at this time of year, which accounted for the fresh flowers. Later they shook hands and said goodbye, and Danny wondered what his father would think of this as he watched them leave the park.

With a full stomach and sluggish with wine, Danny began his search for Aaron's grave. He walked cautiously, fearful of missing the grave and having to begin again. It was like walking down the aisles of a stadium, all seats the same except for the tiny printed number on the backrest. He could tell the graves that were visited regularly by the grass that was worn or the bouquets lying on the stones. He knew that some of the graves were never decorated—the ones that read, "Zwei Unbekant Deutcher Soldaten": "Two Unknown German Soldiers." He searched with a hunter's eye, missed nothing, and eventually found a stone that matched the image in his mind. "Gustav Scholz," it read.

"That is how it will read according to the German records," his grandfather had said. "April 18, 1926–February 1945." Danny knelt by the grave and cupped his chin in his hands, examining the stone like an inspector.

It was late in the afternoon and the sun was a velvet orange that lulled the park to sleep.

"See your brother and speak to him, Danny. It will be your greatest mitzvah," his grandfather had told him. But he couldn't speak, and he couldn't cry either, and he thought that he should. Brothers should cry for each other.

He rose and took a deep breath. Then he stepped back a few rows and sat again. A cool breeze brushed over him as the sun began to fade. In the background he could hear the brakes of the autobus arriving with a few more visitors, perhaps, and he relaxed and lay down. There would be time, he thought, before the last bus. He thought back to when he was thirteen and the night he decided to come here. It was the night of his bar mitzvah, and the entire family was gathered in three rooms of his apartment. He could remember smiling before clinking glasses in toasts and submitting his cheeks to the loving pinches of his uncles and parents' friends.

"Speech!" someone yelled, coaxing Danny to stand on a chair. He stepped onto the seat reeling with pride, a head taller than those around him. All eyes were on him, many filled with tears, as a mock hush filled the room for Danny's words. He recalled how speeches were made and how they always started out with, "Mr. Chairman, Mr. President, and members of whatever organization." He wondered how he would start this speech. The only speech he had given before had been that morning in synagogue. In school he had never been able to summon the courage to go before the class when called on by the teacher. He would stare at her unable to move. His friends would coax him to rise, but he remained solid. Out of school he was never at a loss for words, but in class he would outlast his teacher's request until his eyes filled with tears. He began.

"Mom, Dad, everybody...I want to thank you all for making this one of the most important days in my life, and for making my parents and myself very happy. And thanks for the presents."

The simple speech brought laughter and applause. His mother walked to him and kissed him, as did his father, and people began to talk as before. But Danny had not finished. He continued, and the conversations had quietly stopped.

"The reason that this day is so important is that today I am a man in the eyes of God. I know I'm only thirteen and that I'm not really a man. I can't even get into the movies at night by myself yet. But I know what I want to do when I get older and become a real man. When grandpa was alive, he always told me stories of Aaron and what kind of kid he was. He was the best kid in the world, he said. He always said that Aaron should not be buried in that place, and when I grow up I'm going to bring him home."

A respectful hush had become a deadly silence broken only by the sobs of his mother, which spread to a few of the others. Danny was surprised by the restraint and disappointed by the lack of enthusiasm. He left the chair and began to walk through the room, looking up at the serious faces, some smiling for him, some crying for his parents, and then he ran through the hall to his room, closing the door behind him.

His father came to his room a few moments later and sat on his bed. Danny's face was submerged in pillows. His father began to rub his back gently and soon Danny began to relax.

"Why is my boy crying?" his father asked.

"Don't treat me like a kid. I'm a man now," Danny sobbed defiantly from beneath the pillows.

"We're not treating you like a child, Danny, but you are my boy and always will be my boy even when you're older and have children of your own. Just like your Uncle Fred who calls me his kid brother. I'm over fifty years old, but I'll always be Fred's little brother."

"Really?"

"Sure, and look how old I am."

"I don't believe it."

"It's true. Ask your mother."

"That's amazing."

"It's the same out there," his father continued, pointing behind him, referring to the people in the living room.

"All those people remember little Danny on a bicycle on Ocean Parkway, and they don't see the young man singing the haftorah. Some may never see it." Then with a wink of an eye he said, "Especially your mother."

"Do you?"

"I saw it today, this morning in shule. And I saw it out there. Your speech was very courageous. We were just a little surprised by it, that's all. Sometimes growing up is like a surprise. Don't you remember coming back from camp after the summer, and your friends were taller and had changed? That was only two months since you had last seen them, and they had grown."

"But what do you think, Dad? You never talk about Aaron." His father closed his eyes for a moment and pressed his lips together. His eyebrows raised like they did when he was frustrated or angry, but he wasn't angry. Then he cradled Danny's face and kissed him on the forehead.

"Danny…I don't know…I hope you'll never know what it's like to lose a child." Tears began to form in his father's eyes. "When your brother didn't come back to us, we felt that our lives were over. Your grandfather, God rest his soul, nearly shamed us for our deathlike trance, which we carried for months, and I imagine that it wasn't until you were born that we began to live again."

Danny smiled, proud to be the subject of some joy to his parents. He felt his little face tenderly squashed between his father's hands but had not moved a muscle, knowing how much his father enjoyed touching him.

"We never talked about Aaron because we didn't want to cry anymore. But every time you moved in our midst, I thought of him. Every time I put you over my knee, I thought of how hard I used to spank him and why I stopped. And as I talk to you now, I'm thinking of him, and it gives me great pleasure." His father dropped his hands and spoke more slowly.

"I have trouble sometimes believing that I had sons born on two continents, like I had two lives. But tonight I saw something that connects those lives. I saw something that connects you with your brother. You have courage, Danny, just like your brother, and he would be very proud of you."

"Then it's alright if I go to Italy when I get older?" he asked softly. His father smiled weakly, nodding his head in agreement.

"Yes, Danny, of course it's alright." And he hugged Danny hard, almost hurting him.

"Aaron would like that."

"Dad, could you tell me what happened in Austria?"

"Grandpa already told you."

"I want to hear it from you." His father turned toward the door.

"We have to join the others, Danny."

"It would just take a minute. Please?" His father's shoulders sagged in defeat.

"Alright, let me see..."

The story his father told went like this: "It was winter 1944, and Aaron, who was older than you are now, left the camp where the family was hiding up in the forests of Austria. Soldiers didn't come there. The camp was well hidden, not too far from the Italian border. Something was always going on with Aaron. Making things, fixing things, checking on this and that. He was very talented, and everyone respected him. One day he went to check on the traps, and when he came back with his catch, it wasn't just food. He had a German uniform and, with it, identification papers.

"What are you doing with that?" everyone yelled. "Are you crazy? You want the whole German army here?"

"Aaron wanted to leave the camp for a while to learn of the troops' movements. He'd found the uniform on one of the dead. The Germans were running, but no one knew from whom, the Americans or the Russians. We didn't know if we could leave yet or which direction to run. We didn't want to be liberated by the Russians. I was very upset. I forbade Aaron to leave the camp. A few days passed and one morning after a drenching rain, I woke up, still heavy with sleep, and looked for Aaron. Grandpa said nothing when I asked where he was, and your mother was crying, and then I knew. Aaron had left dressed in the German uniform and armed with a new identity: Gustav Scholz. He left a note reassuring us that he would be back in a few days.

"I was sure he would return," Danny's father said as he finished the story. "He always did."

The cool breeze that soothed Danny before now made him shiver and brought him back to his task at the cemetery. He had been lying on the grass, staring up at the sky unaware of the new arrivals. When he sat up, he was surprised by the presence of a woman just two rows in front of him, kneeling. She was so close he felt like an intruder and wondered if she would be startled by his movements, but he realized that she must have seen him as she approached.

Danny rose and walked slowly to the side to avoid attention. He thought he could see her crying but then recognized that she might be praying. The motions were similar. But could one cry after so many years?

And then he was startled by what he noticed. She was kneeling before the grave of Gustav Scholz. He walked toward her like a visitor looking for a gravestone. He paused and made sure the dates on the stone were the same and then casually walked in front of her. She was neatly dressed and had her hair pulled back. She was a small woman with deep-set, hollow eyes and an arid face void of makeup. Her expression made Danny feel certain that her mind was someplace else. Danny walked farther away and watched from a distance until she rose.

"Who is she?" he wondered. He thought she might be a distant relative from Europe. He considered approaching her and introducing himself. Perhaps it would please her to know they were related, and his parents would be delighted at the coincidence of their meeting. He watched as she arranged the flowers she had placed on the stone and got up to leave. Danny decided to follow her to the bus that was leaving for the village.

He sat in the rear and looked at the woman for whom he had already developed an affection. She sat five rows in front of him and occasionally would turn to look out. He tried to place her in the family. No one came to mind. She might be a distant cousin, he thought. He was elated as he followed her into Mario's. Perhaps she could tell him more about Aaron, what he thought about, what made him laugh. She may even be the last one to have seen him alive.

The waiter asked Danny if he wanted a dessert, jarring him back to the present. He looked at his plate and realized he hadn't eaten much. The food was cold. The man with the little dog had finished his espresso and left. The woman he followed was going through her purse.

"Due cognacs," Danny asked.

"Due?" the waiter asked, holding up two fingers.

"Si, due," Danny answered, wondering whether or not he should greet her in Yiddish or in English. She might not speak a word of English, he thought, but since she was family, surely she would understand some Yiddish. Even poorly spoken Yiddish.

She lifted a compact from her purse, opened it, and examined her face. She was older than he'd thought. She turned her face left to right and back, then raised her head to gain a better view of her neck. That's when Danny saw the gold cross that hung below her neckline, mixing with the striped pattern of her dress.

"Due cognacs," the waiter said, presenting the drinks. Danny said nothing, staring at the cross. He sat at his table, holding the two cognacs like pistols, wondering what the necklace meant. Thoughts raced through his mind. She might have been a girlfriend, then a distant cousin. But she was a Christian. Could Aaron have been in love with a Christian? Did his parents know this?

Danny's visit to the cemetery flashed before him. He thought of the German family who shared their lunch and sat comfortably before the grave of a brother. He thought of Aaron lying there and this woman crying over him and how thankful he was that she did. And he thought of Gustav Scholz and wondered, who cried for him?

Then it hit him. She was not crying for Aaron. She was crying for Scholz. So, who was buried there?

It must be Aaron beneath that stone. He might have been found in the uniform and buried as Gustav Scholz because of the identification papers on his body. But what if he was never found? What if Scholz was discovered by men from his unit who recognized him and brought him back for burial?

Danny slumped in his chair and brought a cognac to his lips, as he watched the woman pay for her dinner. His first sip sent a burning sensation to his throat, taking him by surprise. He must talk to her, he thought. But he couldn't move. Having not eaten, he felt heavy from the wine, pinned to his chair as if someone were pressing on his shoulders. He watched as the woman rose and straightened her dress. She no longer had that look of being in another place, another time. She seemed in control, even satisfied, and it angered him. He thought of her visit to Foto Pass and imagined other visits. She probably comes every year at this time and sits before her brother or husband or lover. It is her best time, he imagined. And he was angry because she had no doubt of who was buried beneath that granite slab and because she had no idea who Aaron was.

He downed the rest of the cognac, hoping his eyes wouldn't water, and struggled to his feet. He headed for her table, leaving the other cognac behind. The woman bent down to pick up her purse, then rose to find herself staring into Danny's eyes. They both stood there, she a bit confused but not threatened, he feeling strangely allied yet frightened from expectation. She looked behind him for some explanation, perhaps, and for a second Danny lost his nerve and wanted to bolt. Then she looked at him again, only this time she smiled, and he extended his hand.

"Guten tag," he said.

Innocence off Broadway

Nathan winced as the waves slammed against the *S.S. Bremen*, which was steaming toward New York. He stretched out his arms and examined his coat for the particles of soot pouring from the stacks. He began brushing away what he could, but stopped when he realized he was only making it worse. His uniform had lost all signs of order and decorum. The sharp creases his pants had when he boarded were gone now, and the blue-gray cloth of his suit was sprinkled with black smudges, the white trim around the sleeves and lapels defiled. Brass buttons that shined only a few days before were slowly being pitted by salt air and seawater. Nathan felt his spray-soaked beard and wondered how long it would be before he could rest and restore the luster to his clothing. His uniform was important to him. He envisioned himself looking for work in his dress grays and for a place to live. Jews weren't commissioned in the Polish army, but Nathan thought that a uniform would set him apart from the rest, and that it would impress the officials at Ellis Island. So he bought one. Officials respect uniforms.

He leaned against the railing looking for some sign of land, some piece of an island, something to tell him the long crossing was over. He saw nothing. As he stared into the heavy mist, he thought back a few days to when he left his father in a village outside of Lvov. He was the last of nine children, his father's favorite. He tried to recall what he felt upon leaving, to savor it, for he knew he would not see his father again. He remembered his father ankle deep in snow, watching him leave for the last time. His father, standing on the platform in his black overcoat and fur hat, didn't try to hide his tears as the train left the station. He was no longer sturdy and confident. Nathan remembered his father's trim black beard, and the heavy eyebrows that caught the snow, which Nathan, as a child, flicked with his finger when his father would let him. He remembered his father waving at the train until he shrank to a black speck, remembered sitting back feeling guilty that he had stopped looking first, while his father was still waving to the rear of the train. He remembered looking out the window again. The speck was still there, though barely visible, and he didn't know if he actually saw him anymore or only imagined he did. He didn't know what his father thought then, but his own feelings were reflected in the tears that rolled down his cheeks as he sat back once more.

The voyage to America challenged the very depth of Nathan's spirit, as the hopes and fears of the steerage seemed to rise and fall with the tilt of the vessel. Rumor followed rumor, hope was crowned with despair, but Nathan held to his faith, his belief in God. It interested him that his father made this same pilgrimage years before, and he wondered what he thought when things looked bad. Did he pray? Did he look to the heavens and pray to the almighty God that he would succeed? His father had declared no allegiance to God, expressing only a passing interest in the mysterious.

Nathan saw himself in synagogue with his father standing by him, and looking up, his father's neck stuck in a starched collar and tie, his bushy eyebrows drawing attention to his face like a blemish. More often than not his father would stare through the window during the service, and Nathan thought he was weighing great things and never bothered him then. Sometimes Nathan would kiss his father's hand. He was not like the other fathers in the neighborhood. Nathan's father had a higher craving, one so high that Nathan had always thought his father wanted to be somewhere else.

The crossing was a difficult one, and the drama of hope that played in thick Jewish accents instilled a realization in Nathan that from now on, whenever he would hear these familiar intonations, a sadness would be renewed. For he had played a similar role for his father whenever he recounted for him the exciting tales of the American West, tales he had gathered from the pages of Karl May, the German novelist.

His father didn't want him to leave. He needed Nathan in the store. But he urged him to go anyway, because he had left once himself and returned with new values and dreams. His father lived in New York for five years, before any of his children were born, on Hester Street, where pushcarts lined the road like long wooden trains carrying tools, cloth, and food. Bearded Jews dressed mostly in black bartered as they had for centuries. Yiddish signs hung from fire escapes on four- and five-story walk-ups, which overlooked muddy streets pockmarked with horse manure and the stench of garbage tossed from apartments above.

Living in a Jewish neighborhood in America had been an experience filled with disappointment, loneliness, and at times even cruelty. But his father left proud, sporting a fine herringbone coat with a black velvet collar, a few hundred dollars, and a spirit that would carry him through many years in Poland.

Nathan knew his father would survive. His father wanted only happiness for him. It was what fathers were supposed to do; otherwise, Nathan would not have even thought about moving. It is the stuff of families that moves us to migrate or remain at home, and there was little thought in Nathan's mind of the difficulty he might face abroad. He had not even considered that he spoke no English, not a word. And he avoided dwelling on his father.

For years his father would receive letters from a place called San Francisco, which was even farther west than those places Karl May described. His father would be relieved that Indians were not a problem there, and amazed that this place even boasted an opera.

The last letter his father read spoke of a dry-goods store Nathan had just opened. He imagined that it looked much like his own, and that Nathan would operate it like he did when he helped his father in his store, and this filled him with a great sense of completion.

He would not read the next few letters, ones that mentioned growth in the business and joy over meeting a Jewish woman from Chicago. And he would not know that Nathan would marry this wonderful woman and that this last son of his would one day have the largest department store in San Francisco, Reich's, and that a bust of himself in a white starched collar and tie, and with those heavy eyebrows, would greet every customer as they entered the main lobby, which stated simply, "Simon Reich, 1810–1882, My Father."

This is the story of my grandfather, Nathan Reich, the story as I heard it from him as a child growing up in San Francisco. I was born Harold Reich to David and Sonya in the year 1919, on a day that brought added joy to my father since on that November evening the Republican Party wrested control from the Democrats and was about to launch a business boom that would help Americans forget the war.

My birth occurred when Nathan was expanding an already successful department store, a plan that did not include his youngest son, David. My father had left the business a few years before. His heart was not in it. He was more comfortable with the written word and had his heart set on writing plays in New York City. And though Nathan did not understand about such things as plays, and though he thought it foolish to leave such a business as this, he understood his son and relented. He gave his blessing, and he gave advice:

"David, if it doesn't work, then come back. Give it two years, three if you need. But don't be a slave to an idea."

My father left San Francisco dreaming of the great Adler and Tomoshevsky portraying his characters on the Yiddish stage. He lived on the East Side, writing his plays in the hope he could bring a new spirit to Yiddish theater, an American spirit. As he looked down from his fifth-story window through the steel railing of the fire escape that hung from the front of the building like a lesion, he saw the Jewish Quarter as a bucket of worms moving about everywhere, occupying every stoop, every curb, and every cobblestone in the street. This is where he wanted to be. From this hardship comes great things, he thought, great theater, though for him it was hard to imagine that in the madness below rested the deposit of the culture and beauty of the people of Israel.

For two years my father wrote his plays and read them before theater owners, the custom then. The plays were not well received. My father felt out of place, and though he was encouraged to continue, he questioned whether he could. He thought he might find a more sympathetic audience uptown where the more sophisticated German Jews lived, but they didn't want his plays either.

"*Quo Vadis* is what they want," an owner told him. "The classics." And downtown, where the Russians lived, he was told the opposite.

"More realism, Reich, more about the Shetle."

"This is realistic," he pleaded. "I write what I know about."

The theater owner smiled condescendingly. "David, no one cares what you know. On that stage they want to see what they know...the Pale, David...Russia. You can write. You've got passion, spirit... Write something else."

It was during a hot summer day at the Thalia, the famous theater of the East Side, where David had a chance to read a new play he had written especially for the Russian audience. He was told that the great Tomoshevsky would be there, along with a small group of players who followed the great actor like children after a promise.

The owners took their seats behind the orchestra. Behind them followed the actors and the actresses. One actress particularly caught David's eye because of her pink shoes. He had never seen pink shoes before, and he thought to himself how free people in the theater are, how different they could be, because they were actors and people expected that of them, and David admired that, and he thought he could write a play about someone in pink shoes, someday.

The theater lights dimmed, and the stage exploded with light. David adjusted his glasses and cleared his throat nervously. He squinted as he tried to see through the blackness, but he saw nothing and finally rested his eyes on the white pages in his hand. His voiced quivered as he began outlining his play before reading it.

As page after page fell to the floor, David relaxed into his play and forgot the audience. He read with feeling, so much that it appeared as if he was trying for a part instead of selling a play. By the time he reached the last line, he was no longer a playwright in the Thalia, but a boy somewhere in the gut of the ghetto on a lonely street, looking toward the rooftops in New York and crying to God for help.

He leaned back in his chair, exhausted, waiting for the lights to come on. When they didn't, he bent over and began gathering his pages from the floor and wondered why there wasn't some polite applause or some movement toward the stage. There was silence as he rose and, shielding his eyes from the lights, tried to spot someone in the darkness. A rush came over him at the idea of meeting Tomoshevsky.

"I'm honored to meet you, sir. I've admired your work, and I hope I didn't displease you with mine," he would say.

Then from the darkness he could hear applause. It was light but firm and clearly from one person, energetic applause that got louder and louder as it came closer to the stage. He could still see nothing, but he could feel excitement race through him. He thought of his grandfather in Russia and wished he were here. This was what it was all about, he explained in his imagination, when someone you respect understands, really understands, like the great Tomoshevsky, and applauds. This is what he tried to explain to Nathan back in San Francisco, who didn't understand about playwriting but understood other things, like dreams.

While David rehearsed in his mind what he would say, he saw a shadow of movement in the aisle, which was still carrying the applause closer to him. As the shadow disappeared into the light, he could see the pointed tips of pink shoes peering from the red border of the cloth that touched them. The light climbed to a thin waist and then to her breasts, which filled an ivory crinoline dress trimmed with crimson velvet. When the light reached her face, the clapping ceased, and David felt a chill come over him. For a moment he was confused, as if he had just placed his hand in extremely hot water after being misinformed that it was ice cold and for those few seconds didn't know which it was. Then he put aside what he knew in his head to be true and wondered why a beautiful girl was applauding in a darkened theater by herself.

And she was beautiful, he thought. Only her small, straight, delicate nose set her apart from those girls depicted on the covers of George Barr McCutcheon's novels. The artists of that day seemed never to paint a girl without an upturned nose, and David thought that if he could have sketched her, he would commission a Christy, Flagg, or Harrison Fisher.

She extended her hand daintily as if she were about to drop a handkerchief, and David reached for it, feeling he had to.

"David Reich," he said.

"I know," she said invitingly. "I liked your play."

"I think you might be the only one who did," he said as he bent down to pick up the few remaining pages. She placed her hand on his shoulder as he leaned down and then removed it.

"I'm sorry," he said, not sure why he was apologizing except that he felt he had made her feel awkward.

"Please…no."

"Don't worry about it…really," he said waving his hand. "I'm writing the same stuff they write, only they can't see it unless it takes place in Minsk." He waved his hand again in disgust, smiling now and deeply hurt, his words not fitting the expression on his face.

He was not sure he was correct in his assumption, so he looked at her. As he did, she bowed her head and looked ashamed, as if she were a willing participant. And then he was sure, soon after he began to read his play, the theater had quietly emptied, leaving him alone to read before a deserted house.

"I'm truly sorry, David," she said softly.

"You have nothing to be sorry for. You stayed." At this she sparkled, almost making David feel uneasy at the quickness of her transition, wondering what part was real and what part was actress. But he liked it nonetheless.

"Who are you, anyway?" he asked.

"Sonya. Sonya Rothschild."

"Rothschild?" David said, implying a connection with the great bankers of France.

"Rothschild, now. Used to be Nemerov," she said with a wink. "I wanted to play uptown. Come," she gestured.

"Where?"

"Outside. Let's go for a walk. We could go to a café. I'm hungry. You must be, too."

"I don't think so."

"Oh, please. It's not good to stay here."

"Oh, I'm not going to stay here. I just..."

"Just what, go home and sit in a lonely sofa chair? You're not the first writer to be made to...get caught like this."

David smiled, enjoying her energy, her hint of a Russian accent, still too strong to break, and smiled at what she almost said. He was feeling sorry for himself and was curious of her attention.

The brilliance of the midday sun reminded David of the lights being turned on in the theater. For a second he felt foolish, like being naked in a summer rain shower. They walked away from the theater and away from the memory of the reading, toward Washington Square. She held his hand, and it felt good. He marveled at the ease of the actress in this social situation—how she just grabbed his hand. A simple girl would not, could not, do that. It would be improper.

As they walked, they exchanged stories of the theater and their childhood, and they laughed. David had not felt this good in a long time. The blow of humiliation was temporarily staved because of this glamorous woman whose close attention soothed him. She lavished praise on him, yet he could not help but believe that it was all an extension of one big joke still not concluded, and for an instant he thought of the young woman who looked at him every morning when he left his apartment building, and whom he acknowledged as interested parties will do. He knew she liked him, and he had similar feelings. He knew that he could trust her and that she was loyal. He knew this despite the fact that no words were ever exchanged except his greeting. And he knew that now he probably would not pay attention to her anymore, and it bothered him. Years later he would picture her leaning out of her first-floor window and shyly acknowledging his greeting with a smile, and he would wonder if she married a butcher or a tailor and if she were happy. He assumed that she was not and that she would have been if he had married her, and he wondered about himself in the same way.

He stopped and turned to Sonya.

"Why would they do that to me? I don't understand it. What if it was a good play and they missed it?"

"That's just it, David," Sonya said. "If it's a good play they won't miss it, and they know that. You'll get another chance, and they will want to see it. Only now they want to play with you."

They were standing in Washington Square, in front of a row of carriages. The familiar odor of horse manure filled the air. Sonya leaned her head on David's shoulder.

"You mustn't give up, David. It truly was a good play. Adler himself would say that."

"Adler? What about the great Tomoshevsky? I can't believe a great actor like that would stoop to such…such nonsense."

"He didn't."

"What do you mean, 'he didn't'? I was there. You were there."

Sonya paused for a moment. "That wasn't Tomoshevsky. It was just another actor."

He turned so that she could see his face. She stayed a comfortable distance from him, careful not to say anything until he gave out what seemed like an uncomfortable laugh, which made her grit her teeth. Then he smiled and grabbed her hand gently.

"Let's walk," he said. They walked in silence, David thinking about what his father had said a few years before, about being a slave to an idea.

My father left the theater a few weeks later to return to San Francisco with his new bride. They moved into Nathan's house, west of Van Ness Avenue, one of those old Gothic-like wooden masterpieces that symbolized pre-fire San Francisco, with its cornucopia of cornices, arches, and bay windows that looked over the bay. My father never returned to his father's department store. Instead, he went to the newspaper, and because he was a Reich, he was hired. And although he would never write another word of fiction, he remained enamored of the written word, and eventually he became assistant to the editor of the third largest paper in San Francisco.

By his side was Sonya. She ran an efficient home, supported her husband, and gave him a son, which pleased him greatly. On the West Coast, as my mother often recounted, she would feel like an immigrant once more, only this time in a place more mysterious and more beautiful than anything she had previously seen. And she would draw comfort from my father and from the different ethnic groups she saw in the streets that reminded her of New York. It was a city at once wild and full of hope, the kind of wildness you would expect from a place built on dreams of gold, where people felt free to do as they wished. But as for my mother, she no longer wore things like pink shoes.

Segura's Hand

Tonight will be different. There will be no sparring in the gym and no familiar face in the ring this time. Tonight it's the sports arena. There will be programs, probably a reporter from the *Toledo Blade*, and there will be people. Lots of people.

I cradle my face in my taped hands in the dressing room, gazing at the tiled floor. I begin counting the little squares to stop my heart from pounding. I think of my father for a moment.

"Craziness, this boxing. Mishugas. Jewish boys don't fight." I remember the day I found a tennis racket on my bed. A smile comes to my face.

I stand up, shaking my arms, and move my slender frame into a dancing pattern in front of a cracked mirror that leans against the wall. It leans there as a silent cheerleader to the shadow-boxers. Pip...pip...pah... My hand shoots two jabs and follows with a hook. I like myself in the mirror. Good form. "He pretty," they say. "Pretty for a white boy." I'm the only white boy on the PAL team this year, but it doesn't bother me. There's no towel-snapping in the showers, but I'm comfortable. "The white dude." Just different.

Pettaway pats me on the can as he dances by, jabbing an imaginary opponent. I acknowledge with a nod. Tonight we're close. He moves on, slipping his lanky brown body into a lavender and white satin robe. He's ready to go up. The door opens a few inches, and a bald head appears.

"Pettaway," it says coldly and disappears. I watch a confident middleweight half-dance, half-walk out the door. The noises barge in momentarily and then vanish when the door clicks shut. The noises start my heart pounding again. This is for real. The minutes pass too quickly as my mind carries the battle of my fists. There is a coldness to this moment.

Again the door opens, allowing a fresh burst of noise to enter. The bald head appears expressionless, calling me. It's time.

Unattended, I snake through dirty aisles to a chair near the ring. No paths are made for amateurs. Not this one. The lights are bright and hot at ringside. Heavy smoke fills my eyes with tears. Nervously I blink to wash the smoke away, but my eyes cloud. "What if I can't see?" I think. Cautiously I rub my eyes with the sleeve of my robe. The satin is cold on my pupils.

I look up to a joyous scene. Pettaway is smiling broadly, exposing his mouthpiece like a jubilant horse, and for a moment I feel confident of winning. Across the ring I see my opponent entering. The noise is loud, but I hear mostly the creaking in the wooden stairs. I count each step. My corner is buzzing with instruction but I hear little.

Waiting for the bell, I gaze into the blackness of the arena, pricked only by the striking of matches. I'm all alone now.

The bell sounds and reverberates in the pit of my stomach. I shuffle to the center of the ring, and now after six months of training, the fight begins. Six months of the pungent smell of soiled trunks and jocks. Six months of sweat, red welts, and intermittent pissing of blood from too many body blows. Six months of lonely bus rides after school, to another loneliness of dressing separately while the others share hopes and dreams of title fights. Hope is the only thing that flourishes in this stale air.

Stiff jabs to my head shake loose whatever fears I have, and I begin to return staccato-like jabs. Soon, he catches me with an overhand left. I'm not shaken, just surprised. He hits me easily. His arms seem long and hard to avoid. Again he lands an overhand left, just before the round ends. This one goes to Segura.

Between rounds my coach yells at me. "Circle right, circle right! He's hitting you!"

I nod.

"Understand?" he asks.

I nod again, but I don't understand. My breathing is hard. I walk out again to meet the stocky Mexican. It seems like a repetition of the first round. I can't get started. He seems so far away, yet all I see is his right hand in my face. My arms feel heavy. I draw on everything I've been taught and begin dancing, but I grow weary as he seems to gather strength. I'm waiting for the bell to ring, already thinking about the next round. The next will be different.

I slump in my stool waiting for the final bell. Coach Carr continues his lecture. I nod mechanically, wondering if I can make it through the final round. The bell sounds, and I meet Segura, knowing that only a knockout will save this for me. This time I slip a stiff jab and embrace him in the haven of a clinch.

The cheering becomes clearer now. I can even hear my name a few times, and I summon what strength I have left. Pip! Pip!—two hard jabs to his nose bring blood. The sight of the crimson excites me. As the blood trickles down his face, my strength rushes upward and urges me to wage battle. In a flurry of punches we exchange everything we have, catching each other flush on our jaws. It doesn't hurt. I take his biggest punch, and it doesn't hurt. I feel good. I feel like I can take whatever he has to give. My left arm is down confidently. My right hand is cocked, ready to throw a final blow. The crowd is cheering, and I think it's for me. I want the round to last. I'm tired. Dead tired. But I'm stalking. It feels good to hit and be hit. Nothing hurts. This is going to be my fight. I can feel it. Suddenly, disappointingly, the bell sounds the end. We slump into each other's arms as tradition demands, though it seems to come naturally.

My corner removes my mouthpiece, and I'm surprised by the blood that covers it.

"Why the hell didn't you circle right? You circle right on a lefty," my coach says. I sit there with a smile on my face. I understand now. I hadn't realized I was fighting a lefty. My expression confuses the coach. He's more depressed than me.

"Next time, kid."

I nod, but I know that there won't be a next time, for I didn't come here to be a champion. I came here simply to fight. To hit and be hit. To hit so hard that someone would bleed, even me. I came to throw away the commandments that say, "We Jewish boys don't fight. We abhor violence, so we don't fight."

And my father, that loving, generous, sweet man, will wonder why I can smile through a swollen, distorted face. He will be angry at this "craziness," but it will only reflect my anger bottled up for so long. I came here to fight that kid in Brooklyn who years ago pounded me daily after school, while I did nothing.

And as I stand in the middle of the ring, beginning to feel the pain, I am unmindful of the referee raising Segura's hand in victory.

Short-Timer

One more. Just a wake-up. One day. I've been awake for an hour, I think. Too much excitement. Reveille will be in an hour. Holiday will piss and moan all the way to the shower. Hysong will be silent, like a time bomb. I never know what he's thinking, but he's smart. He just doesn't let you know too much. Speaks in spurts. Intelligent spurts—facts and opinions, mostly opinions. Sometimes I understand them. Sometimes I don't, but I don't ask too many questions. I'm going to lie here and take my time.

For a thousand days I've been filling in those tiny squares on the naked girl taped to the inside of my locker. I remember when I counted backwards for the first time. I was still at Fort Sill. Nine hundred twenty-five days to go. It'll never come, I thought. And here it is. My last two breakfasts in Germany, then to the bahnhof. The ritual I was waiting for. How many times have I driven with someone to the bahnhof to say goodbye after laughing and drinking beers, drawing disapproving stares from the locals? "Americans, too loud."

Now it's my turn. Going back to the land of the round doorknobs. Four or five guys will take me there. They'll get a morning off from their first sergeants. It fits nowhere in the regulations, but is winked at even when the morning becomes all day and three or four of them come back to the Kaserne, drunk. We'll drink and promise to write. Maybe I'll even come back as a civilian, I say. And I mean it. But I probably won't. None of us do.

I remember the night I arrived, when the ship came into Bremerhaven. We couldn't leave until morning. I wanted to see what a foreign country looked like, so I walked on deck and leaned over the rail. The mist in the air was like in a late 1940s British movie. The first thing I saw was a German policeman walking slowly on the dock in a heavy gray gabardine coat with a high-brimmed hat, holding a German shepherd by a leash. This also looked like something in a movie.

In the morning I took the train from Bremerhaven by myself, orders tucked in my inside pocket. "Don't lose the orders," they said back in Oklahoma. From the train station in Ansbach, I took a cab to Barton Barracks.

No one was there. Well, not exactly. Lieutenant Bird was there from Company C 1st Missile Battalion, 33rd Artillery, my new unit. And Johnny Simmons from the 210th Artillery Group, and Tommy Townsend, the battalion clerk from the 33rd.

That was all. The rest of the battalion was in Grafenwoehr, playing war games for a month. Lieutenant Bird was in charge, and Tommy Townsend was there to fill out the morning reports. He was a short-timer. He had seventy-six days to go. He wasn't tall, just a bit taller than me, but he was solidly built. His hair was longer than mine—I was still letting it grow back, and he was immune from criticism at this point. "Short," he would sputter at the drop of a hat. "Short," a word that would become the most revered in the military, at least for those who were not bent on making a career of it.

I like to think of those twenty-odd days of this incredible freedom that I fell into as my "salad days" in this man's army. I awoke when my eyes opened and not because of a whistle in my ear. I unknowingly hatched my reputation there and then, so that Tommy Townsend was able to slip me gently into his job as battalion clerk, thereby saving his boss, the sergeant major, the task of finding someone to fill his shoes.

"What's he like?" I asked.

"Big and loud, but basically a pussy. The cooks are terrified of him. But they're afraid of their own shadow. This office terrifies them. The cooks are lower than whale shit in the scheme of things. All they do is cook and drink."

"Can you type?" he asked.

"Sure."

"Army regulations call for forty-five words a minute, no mistakes. Can you do that?"

"I don't know."

So Townsend tested me that second or third day after deciding that he liked me enough. He watched with amazement as I pounded out forty-four words, one short, in one minute without a mistake. Amazed, because I was typing with two fingers.

"Is that the way the army taught you?"

"The army didn't teach me. I'm artillery. They taught me how to shoot Howitzers."

Townsend laughed at the thought of the sergeant major's reaction to the two fingers.

"He won't give a shit just so long as you do your work and don't get beat up by the Krauts or the MPs. At your size, you sure ain't gonna beat anyone else up."

"Thanks."

I was, essentially, the battalion clerk elect. My honeymoon period ended with the roar of trucks pouring through the Barton Barracks gate in January 1965. Sergeant Major Vall looked at me, gave me a "harrumph," and that was that. The next morning I was sitting next to Tom as before, continuing to learn the office routine, but now with the battalion commander and the major walking in and out. It wouldn't take long before I became comfortable with military brass.

The battalion commander, Colonel R. W. Haddox, like any other commander, has no real idea what is going on with the men because he has no close contact. He depends upon his lieutenants and captains in the batteries and upon the sergeant major. If an event occurs overnight, it is the duty of the sergeant major to apprise Lieutenant Colonel Haddox of the news. Vall relishes news like a Hollywood gossip, and he likes local news best. Vietnam doesn't hold much interest for him.

"Good morning, sir," he might say, standing up as the colonel arrives. I get him a cup of coffee. Black.

"Well, Sergeant Major, what have you got?"

"Well, sir, it appears that one, Specialist Four, 'Hey-zoos' Rodriguez" —and here he might drag out "Hey-zoos" instead of calling him "Jesus" —"in a state of high inebriation, saw fit to strike one, Sergeant E Five Lewis J. Sampson, about the head and shoulders, causing said sergeant severe trauma and thereby causing the MPs to seek immediate care for him at the Nuremburg Hospital."

The colonel listens to these reports quietly and then leans on the sergeant major for advice. Vall is wise to infractions of this sort, and the colonel relates well with him as they are the only two in the battalion old enough to have served during World War II.

"Who is this, Rodriguez?"

"Company B, sir."

It is here where the critical part of the process begins, where the review, or the critique, or the subjective analysis is provided. If Vall likes you, you might receive an article 15, a slap on the wrist. If he doesn't, it could result in a summary court martial. A summary court martial is less than a court martial, but serious enough. If he likes you, Vall might talk up your merits and the colonel can then suggest the article 15. If Vall doesn't like you, he might begin with the sordid history, embellishing the tale of the soldier and working each other into an emotional state. This would signal to the colonel to take a tougher stand. By the time I had filled in another ninety squares on my naked girl, I could predict the soap opera that would unfold in the colonel's office.

Soon the night duty sergeant will walk down the hall blowing a whistle and shouting for us to get up. I still have to do the morning report and show the new guy the ropes. I realize that I haven't thought of Tommy Townsend in a long time.

Every morning each unit in the army produces a morning report and sends it to higher headquarters; eventually it makes its way to Washington. It gives the government a picture of the Army's strength to a man. It's the most taxing part of my job, because mistakes are not tolerated. There can be no erasures or cross-outs. Each morning I receive reports from four companies and fold the information into mine. Then I anxiously walk the report over to the 210th Artillery Group and wait for the verdict. Generally it is accepted. When it isn't, I have to retype it. I can't stand it when I have to retype.

We have 360 men in the 33rd and all are on base except one. Mandeville is his name, and he is at Manheim, a military prison.

"Who's this guy in the box?" I asked Tommy when I first began typing these reports.

"Spec four Mandeville killed a girl before I got here. He'll be in that box long after you're gone."

"Shit. Murder?"

"Yeah. But he won't do more than twelve years and then the Krauts get him, I think. Or something like that."

So I type a "1" every day in a certain box, which represents Mandeville, and I wonder about him every time I enter that number. Every day I imagine him in a prison cell waiting without the benefit of a naked girl with boxes to fill in, for he doesn't know how many boxes there are. I don't wonder if he's a nice guy. I only think about what he might have done.

My arrival at the 33rd really began when the troops returned from "Graf." That is when, in an instant, 360 men were milling about the Kaserne. Everything was new and different, yet in a very short time it was all familiar. I instantly had three new roommates, and it took as long as it took for the next new soldier to appear at the gate to feel comfortable in my new surroundings, for as far as the new guy was concerned, I could have been here ten years.

The barracks are like the Waldorf compared with the wooden shacks in the States. Barton Barracks is an old German Army Kaserne that is on loan to the U.S. Army. The barracks are two stories tall, built of stone and concrete and heated by steam. Instead of a long hall filled with thirty men, four men share a room. The Germans live a more civilized existence than we do back home.

It's almost reveille. The guys are still sleeping. I wonder what will be the most fun, going to the bahnhof or taking the train to Frankfurt? What about the flight to the States? Or in New York, the subway from downtown? I wonder where they'll let me off. I look up at the ceiling. In a couple of days the ceiling will be in New York. It's over. I think of the guys who left girlfriends they met in bars downtown, the guys who promised to write and don't. And I think of the guys who were so lonely they got married quickly and moved off base. But there's no one for me to say goodbye to. I remember comforting girls who called asking me if I had heard from their boyfriend. I can't tell them anything, because I don't know anything.

Sergeant Major Vall has red hair sprinkled with gray. You can hardly tell it is red anymore, because it's a crew cut, flat on top and close to the skin. His face is reddish, too clean-shaven, like it would be out of order if a whisker appeared. His green fatigues, always pressed and too green as he no longer works in the field. A sergeant major's job is a desk job. At the close of work one day in my first week, Vall was whispering something to my first sergeant, Sergeant E Eight Crane. Crane turned to me and motioned me to follow him. I looked at Vall and he gave me a friendly wink. Crane is about five feet, ten inches tall, with a reddish complexion from drinking too much. He goes on binges once in a while, so drunk he disappears for days. I was instructed to leave it out of the morning report. An example of how the Army looks after its own. One of those things not discussed.

Crane spoke in monotones and never smiled. He always appeared angry and I thought to myself that he was just that. He spoke in short, flat sentences and disliked me because, though I was in his company and under his jurisdiction, he felt powerless to push me. He couldn't give me guard duty or k-p as I was in the sergeant major's office. Soon after I arrived he brought me to the basement of Company B where the arms room was located. Spec Four Myron Silver was in charge. Silver was thin, had sharp features, and looked smart. He was busy taking in rifles from GIs and placing them in the cage.

"Silver!" Crane said a bit loudly.

"Yeah, Top?"

"Sergeant Major wants you two to meet. Rosengart here is Jewish." With that, Crane departed. I stood there awkwardly, giving Silver a slight smile. Silver smirked.

We shook hands.

"You R.A. or U.S.?" Silver asked, wondering if I was drafted or enlisted.

"R.A.," I said, uncomfortable and embarrassed, knowing he was probably drafted.

"R.A?"

"Yeah, don't ask. It's a long story."

Silver shrugged.

"Why do they want us to meet, ya think?" I asked.

"Because you're a Jew. Most of them never met one. Also I'm outta here in forty-one days and a wakeup," he said with a smile.

I learned something about Silver that day. He was going home with a large stash of money he had acquired as the Baron Rothschild of the 33rd. He loaned money. Everyone borrowed from him, including the officers.

"They probably sent you here to take over my business."

"Business?" I said.

"Yeah. They call me 'First National' around here. 'First National Silver.'" I stared at him, not comprehending.

"I loan money," he said more emphatically.

"I don't have any money to lend," I said.

"You do if you have five bucks. A week after payday most guys have pissed away their monthly salary on booze and pussy. They come to me and ask if they can borrow five bucks till payday. Payday comes and they pay me back seven-fifty. Ten bucks gets me fifteen, and so on. Get it?"

"That's fifty percent interest. They put you under the jail for that."

"That's the Army. Hey, I didn't make the rules. It's army-wide."

"I get it."

Later I learned that Sergeant Needham from Mississippi, a black sergeant, re-enlisted. He hated the Army, but was making too much money to quit. He was the banker for the black soldiers.

I think about Silver and remember my trip over. I was on a Navy ship leaving the Brooklyn Navy Yard. We stopped in Norfolk to pick up a few hundred Seabees, then continued on to Rota, Spain, to drop them off, and finally through the English Channel to dock at Bremerhaven. The seas were rough and the boat swayed from side to side. Lots of GIs got sick, and many who didn't fought hard to keep it down. On a particularly rough stretch through the English Channel, an announcement came over the loudspeakers instructing us to use the paper bags draped over the handrails situated over the gutters on the walkways. For many it was too late. The hardest part was walking towards the dining room, thinking of food and seeing the vomit in the gutters rolling back and forth as the ship rocked through the channel. You couldn't let go of your tray, or it would slide off the table and onto the floor. When I arrived at the mess hall one evening, it looked like a food fight in a silent movie. GIs were slipping on food, trays were flying, and food was piling on food already spilled. Food was on the floor, on the benches, on the tables, most of it no longer on trays. It was hard to tell food from vomit. The mood was somber. GIs were holding on to their trays with one hand and eating with the other. Yet I found myself laughing, and hustled out of there hungry rather than try to eat.

We crossed in January. Every day twice a day we were ordered on deck for recreation. Recreation was standing still in the cold wet wind complaining about the cold. It didn't matter if it was a clear day. The wind picked up the waves and threw them over the deck in a fine spray. If you don't work on a ship, then you merely stand around and after a few days tension builds. The only real entertainment on board was a snack bar, where candy and toiletries were offered. By the seventh day the stock was running thin. I was walking back to my bunk when I saw a GI drinking a bottle of Aqua Velva. I lay on my bunk and remembered my Uncle Irving telling me about the soldiers coming through Stanislav in Poland during the First World War: "Every week, it was the Russians, then the Poles, then the Ukrainians or the Austrians, and they were starving. So I went to my grandmother and bought chocolate one time. She had a little store, you know. She sold thread mostly. Well, when the soldiers came through again, I sold the chocolate to them. I was ten years old."

I went down to the snack bar and bought all the candy. The cigarettes were already gone. That evening after dinner, word got around that Private Rosengart had candy for sale. I sold out in two days. It was my introduction to high finance and a harbinger of what was to come, and what an uncle taught about survival during difficult times in a village in Poland, would come to aid a private in the U.S. Army fifty years later.

It's drizzling outside as usual. Germany in March. Still cold. Still wet. We drag ourselves outside for reveille in various states of dress, all unkempt. Shirts are hanging out. Hats are on backwards. Some can't find their field jackets. The night-duty sergeant is in the middle of the parade field but we can't see him. It's still dark here. It's always dark here, it seems. He calls out to each battery. Each answers, "All present and accounted for, Sergeant."

"Fuckin' Army," Bogdalek mutters.

"Short," someone else says.

I smile to myself. I really am short. Tomorrow I leave.

We hear the needle of the record player over the sound system.

"C'mon, I'm freezing my balls off," Ippolito says.

Reveille is played, the flag raised. No one can see it. No one cares.

"Dismissed!" shouts the NCO, and we all muster back into the barracks. Some go back to sleep till seven-thirty. Others shower and go to the mess hall. Some go to the snack bar on post for a breakfast they have to pay for. It makes them feel like they're home for a while.

I inch down the chow line at the mess, sliding my aluminum tray. I raise it up and a cook dumps a large spoon of scrambled eggs in one of the three triangles. No one ever asks how you like them. I hear that in the Navy and Air Force you can place an order. Murphy next to me raises his tray for "shit-on-a-shingle." It's off-white gravy with some kind of meat in it.

"Goddammit, Murph, how can you eat that shit?" I ask.

He doesn't even look up, grabbing two biscuits. He probably never ate so well in his life. Murph is from Wrens, Georgia. He told me once that the Army took out all his teeth after basic training and gave him a new set.

It's later in the morning at the office. The report is done. Colonel Haddox walks in. He is from the brown-boot Army and fought in the big one after Pearl Harbor. He wears the same boots now, only they've been dyed black. He's getting out soon because he's been passed over for full bird. He won't be humiliated again.

He comes in loud with a, "Good morning," to the sergeant major and a nod to me and enters his office, which is attached to ours. He leaves the door open, allowing Vall to knock and enter. I fetch his coffee. I place his coffee on his desk and turn to leave.

"You're leaving today, I hear," says Haddox.

"No, sir. Tomorrow, sir." He smiles. We've had one conversation in the two years that I've been here. It was in Graf where we spent a month shooting the "Honest John," our outdated missile system. It has a range of eleven miles and takes about twenty-five minutes to get off a round. It's large and transports on a Studebaker truck, I'm told. I was driving the colonel in a Jeep from the field back to Headquarters Battery.

"You're Jewish, aren't you, Rosengart?" he asked.

"Yes, sir."

"Both parents?"

I wanted to laugh but I didn't dare.

"Yes, sir."

"Did your father serve in World War II?"

"He was in his thirties when the war broke out, sir, and he had two kids. He wasn't drafted, but he was a volunteer fireman."

"Hmmm." We drove on a bit as I remember, and then he said to me, "I'm gonna miss this tank trail." Shooting the "Honest John" was probably going to be his last act involving anything with artillery. "I'd like to say goodbye to it. What do you think, Rosengart?"

"I think that's a good idea, sir."

I turned the Jeep around and drove a mile toward the tank trail and stopped. Colonel Haddox stood up holding onto the top of the windshield with his left hand and placed his right hand in salute.

"Goodbye, tank trail." He sat down. "Thank you, Rosengart."

Back in the office on my last full day, Haddox wishes me well.

During the day I'm mostly showing the new guy his duties. It frees me up to get out. I'm already gone to the sergeant major. He's polite but pays no attention to me. He's not emotionally involved. Like a doctor with his patients, he sees too many soldiers changing job status too often. It's the Army way. I'm essentially out of a job and off the grid and I like it that way. If I want to leave I tell Vall, and he nods.

My locker is clean. I've thrown stuff out from the bottom and top shelf and cleared out my footlocker. I'm resting on my bed when Ridley walks in. He's from Carthage, Mississippi, like Sergeant Needham. When I learned from the roster that these two guys were from the same small town, it seemed to me as if it would have been a wonderful coincidence for them.

"So what?" Ridley said, when I asked him about it.

"What'dya mean, 'so what?'"

"He's a nigger."

"You don't talk to each other?"

"What for?"

I remember when he saw a picture of my girlfriend on my desk. She has dark skin.

"She looks like a nigger," he said, laughing. I laughed, too, feeling uncomfortable. Why was I so worried about his feelings? Or was I uncomfortable because I lacked the courage to call him on it? This uncompromising dislike he had for blacks trumped what would have normally been a stroke of good fortune, having someone from your town with whom to share the misery of Army life and the memories of home. I imagined how wonderful it would have been for me to have someone from my own block in New York. But to Ridley, Needham was nothing more than a distraction. They saw each other every day and hardly talked. And when they did, it was in the line of duty. Nothing from home.

"You're going home, you little fuck." He gives me five.

"I love you, too, Ridley."

"What are you gonna do when you get back?"

"Probably work with my father."

"That's cool."

"You're short, too."

"I don't know who told you," he joked.

Ridley is six feet, strong, and quick-witted. His hair is black and combed back. It looks like it should have a comb stuck in it.

"I have to tell you the truth, Rid."

"What's that?"

"I ain't gonna miss you."

He turns to leave, picks up the framed picture of my girlfriend, places it back down on my desk, and laughs. I don't expect to see him at the bahnhof.

Later in the afternoon, I'm walking across the parade field headed for the library. I need to say goodbye to the librarian. I spent Christmas Eve with her and another GI from the 57th Artillery Group sitting around a small record player listening to Bing Crosby, Nat King Cole, and Perry Como. It was here that I was introduced to eggnog and fell in love with Christmas. I felt like Van Johnson in a World War II movie, with the librarian as my Jane Wyman. It was like being in the States for a while. There were no slogans, like "Zero Defects" or "Loose Lips Sinks Ships," on the wall. Just books.

The library is closed. It's after four, and I'll be gone in the morning. I head back to the barracks. A bunch of the guys want me to go downtown to celebrate, but I beg off. Holiday and I drive to Rothenburg to eat out. Dressing in civilian clothes to go to restaurants gets me through this. We talk about the future and the past twenty-four months, and we laugh. It all seems funny now. I remember not being able to get through *Catch 22* because it wasn't funny to me. Not when you think you're living it.

"Remember when Haddox wanted a life-size lion constructed?" Holiday asks.

"Remember? Where the hell do you think I sit?" Holiday laughs. Our unit insignia includes a resting lion on a red background and the colonel decided one day that we should have a lion made.

"Yes, sir," Vall said, closing the colonel's door. "Pig shit," he said under his breath.

"Rosengart, the colonel wants a life-size lion made up."

"For what, Top?"

"Never mind for what. Just help me figure how to do it."

For days we thought about it and for days Sergeant Vall hoped that Haddox would forget about it. He didn't.

We came up with the idea that the medics could make a lion out of gauze and some kind of glue.

"I remember walking into the office to pick up the major to take him somewhere, and this fuckin' lion is sitting on the floor. What did they make the hair out of?"

"They used a mop."

"Whatever happened to that thing?" Holiday asks.

"It sat in the colonel's office for two weeks until the inspector general came through, and he didn't want to be caught dead with it."

"I remember now. I took it to supply and they drove it around Nuremburg for the whole day so it wouldn't be on base. Fuckin' guys are dying in Nam and this schmuck wants a lion in his office made out of gauze."

We head back to Ansbach and I turn in. I've got a wake-up.

I'm surprised by the whistle. It's not like yesterday when I woke early and couldn't go back to sleep from the excitement. Reveille. Screw it, I'm short. Hysong and Holiday try to wake me and I tell them I'm sleeping. I think of the bahnhof and I'm excited all over again. I picture my ride downtown, the sendoff at the train station and the train to Frankfurt. It's today. I'm actually leaving.

The door opens and it's Sergeant Crane.

"On your feet, Rosengart! You're not home yet. Get your ass out there!"

"Just about to do that, Top," I say grabbing my pants and putting my field jacket over my T-shirt, boots in hand.

"Don't be a wise-ass."

In a few seconds I'm in formation in the dark, putting on my boots. Bogdalek is complaining as usual, this time in a mock baby voice.

"I don't want to play here anymore. I want to go home."

"Fuckin' Army!"

"Short!"

"What are you doing here?" Holiday asks.

"Crane," I say.

"Asshole."

I say goodbye to the colonel and the sergeant major. Hysong, Holiday, Brownell, and Rodriguez drive me down to the bahnhof. I haven't seen Ridley. I walk past Sergeant Crane's room and slip my naked girl poster from my locker under his door. The ride downtown is loud. I'm taking the jokes and laughing, yet thinking much about what I just left behind. But the sendoff will be good. We rehash our experience together and begin drinking beer at ten. As we exchange old stories, I think of how lucky I've been. I didn't get sent to Korea or Nam. And I didn't have to load Howitzers like I was trained, because I met Tommy Townsend one cold day in January, when everybody was gone. I didn't have k-p and I didn't pull guard duty.

"You never had guard duty, you lucky bastard. You had it easy," Brownell says.

"Yeah, I did, but it was in basic and AIT," I answer with a smile, referring to basic training and advance infantry training. I recall my experience with guard duty during basic at Fort Dix. It was two hours on, four hours off. When we were off, we slept in the guardhouse. I walked my first two hours and then was relieved and went back to sleep. Private Friedman ROTC, a six-monther, was hungry.

"Rosengart, you hungry?"

"Yeah."

"Let's sneak over to the snack bar and get a hamburger."

"We can't leave our post," I said.

"We're off for four hours. Who's gonna know?"

I thought about it. And it made sense. No one was here but sleeping soldiers. Plus, who was going to check to see that we were sleeping? If anything, they would check to see that we were not sleeping while on guard. They weren't going to come in to see if our eyes were closed.

"Sure, what the hell," I said. We carefully looked outside. No one was around. So we walked over to the snack bar and ordered hamburgers, fries, and Cokes.

As I enjoyed my greasy burger, I caught a glimpse of Sergeant Walker not five tables away from us doing the same thing. Sergeant Walker was our drill instructor. He made out the duty roster and loved his job. He especially loved putting his face in mine and yelling commands, and I remember being both impressed and stunned when I heard him say in a sentence, "It will behoove you mens."

"We're screwed," I said.

"Why?" Friedman asked, with his mouth full of fries.

"Don't look now, but to your left, about four or five tables down, is Sergeant Walker."

"Does he see us?"

"Oh, yeah, and he's smiling."

"That's good."

"Bullshit, it is!" I said.

"Listen. Let me do all the talking. Got it?"

"What are you gonna say?"

"Don't worry about it. Is he coming over?"

"No, he's finishing up and they're going. Maybe it's okay."

Only it wasn't okay. The next morning we were summoned to the captain's office. It was Saturday, parade day, and Captain Turner was dressed in his dress blues. Hanging from his side was his sword in its sheath, and the top of his black boots reached to just below the knee. He was born at the wrong time and for the wrong war. He looked at Friedman and me and then left us in his office for a moment.

"Is this guy playing dress-up?" Friedman asked. "He looks like Hermann Goering." I stifled a laugh.

"Remember, let me do the talking," Friedman said.

We could hear the click of the metal taps on his boots as he returned to his office with Sergeant Walker. He looked over some paper. I thought we might go to jail, and I was scared.

"Do you know how serious this is, gentlemen?"

"Yes, sir," Friedman said. I was happy he was talking. Maybe the captain would just yell at us.

"Leaving your post is the most serious violation of Army rules. Soldiers' lives are at stake."

"Yes, sir."

"Then tell me, Private Friedman and Private Rosengart, tell me why you left your post," he prompted in a calm, controlled voice.

"It was the pork," Friedman said. I looked straight ahead, not at Turner for a moment. The pork? I wondered.

"The pork?" the captain asked.

"Yes, sir. The pork," Friedman said.

"I don't understand, Friedman."

"Well, sir, we're Orthodox Jews, and we are not allowed by our faith to eat pork. And last night as we walked down the chow line, I couldn't recognize the meat and I asked the cook if that was pork they were serving, and he said yes. We didn't eat any dinner, and we were afraid we might pass out while on guard duty. We weren't sure which would be worse, to get some sleep and maybe gather strength that way, or just get a bite, so we could stand guard when it was our turn."

Turner was stunned. He looked at Sergeant Walker and Walker said nothing. I was stunned as well. Maybe this is why we've been persecuted for 5,000 years, I thought. This is too much. He'll never buy it.

He bought it. Captain Turner walked around to his desk and picked up the papers again. Then he turned around and looked out on the parade field.

"Friedman, Rosengart, you should have told someone of this. Sergeant Walker here could have handled this for you."

He actually bought it.

"I'm going to forget this, this time. But don't ever do anything like this again. Do you read me?"

"Yes, sir."

"Yes, sir," I said.

"Dismissed."

We walked back to the barracks, careful not to talk or show any excitement until clearly out of sight.

"What if he checks the menu from last night?" I asked.

"Who gives a shit? That's what the cook told me."

"But we didn't have pork last night."

"That's what the cook told me, I'll say. Maybe the cook thought I liked pork, and he wanted to make me feel good. Don't worry about it. This guy would rather play Cowboys and Indians than deal with this shit."

Friedman was right. It was over and we got out of it. I was close to him those remaining weeks in basic. I remember feeling sad when we left, he for AIT and home and me for AIT and a thousand days. And I thought of the captain. He was sensitive to our imagined plight and I felt guilty, because he appeared foolish to me with his sword and pearl handle pistol and took his job seriously, and part of that job was caring about his command.

It's close to noon and we've been drinking beer for two hours. As a train pulls into the station, my heart begins to race. I'm nervous all of a sudden, but the joking and the toasting relaxes me.

"It's the schnellzug!" Brownell says, a bit tipsy. I look at these guys and realize something as we talk of keeping in contact and getting together in the States. I realize how close I am to them at this moment and how only they will know exactly how it was to be here. I also know that it is this mutual dislike of the Army that unites us. That is the glue, and when we part, there won't be that glue anymore. We'll all have a new freedom and a new direction, and there won't be this anger every day. As I hug each one of them and promise to write, I throw my duffel bag with the help of one of the guys, jump onto the now slow-moving train inching out of the bahnhof, and know that I will never again come back here, nor will I ever again cross off a day on a calendar.

Time Enough for a Party

The mirror mocks me as I stare at the pimples that define my face. I imagine a great healing machine that will dry them instantly, drinking up excess oils and leaving my skin clear. I haven't had a Hershey Bar in two years. I take more time in front of the mirror tonight because it's New Year's Eve and I want to look good. Through the bathroom door I hear the canned laughter from the "I Love Lucy" show, and I make out my mom and pop mumbling something about the party I'm going to tonight. They don't know where it is, and I don't tell them. I hardly tell them anything of my social life.

While I shave, I think of the new, drab olive suit that lies on my bed. It's a very popular color this year, and the cool guys are wearing it in school. It's the first suit I've worn without cuffs. The pant length is too long, longer than the way the colored kids wear them. I wish they were shorter.

For a few minutes I stand in the living room with my parents and watch Lucy get in trouble. There's no need to hurry.

"Is that the new suit?" my mother asks.

"Yeah, Ma. What do you think?"

"Very nice," she says, as she touches the sleeve. She means it.

"Well, I gotta go." I turn to leave. "Don't wait up either. I'll be late."

"Have a good time," my dad says. They're both smiling, happy their son is going out.

"No coat?" my mother asks. "Wear a coat. It's cold."

"It's not cold," I say to cut off any ensuing battle.

I hear my mother say resignedly, "You stinker," as I open the door. "He should wear a coat. It's freezing, Sigmund," as it closes. I can picture my father shrugging as I walk into the cold evening.

The walk to the subway is frigid, as the wind wraps around the buildings and pierces my clothes. But soon I drop a token in the turnstile and catch the "A" train after it rocks into the station. I sit in a half-empty car.

Faces facing, each expressionless as they stare into each other's exterior or read the posters that promise to cure their colds, make them rich, or make them beautiful. "No credit?" "Can't get insurance?" "Lost your job?" "Take one." But there are no slips. And the ruins of rush hour pave the floor. *The Daily News* lies at my feet, rich with photos that say everything about us, and Miss Subway this month is Rita Gonzales.

Local stations flash by like small villages as the Eighth Avenue Express carries me toward major cities. I look to the window to read the number on one of the stations. 86th Street. No, 81st. Can't make it out. We're going too fast, like a thousand miles an hour on these screaming metal wheels.

My eye catches another eye, and I look away. Again I look, and now I try hard not to stare at him directly. I remember someone who chased me around the IRT station last year with his fly open, simply because I stared at him. A man sits with his lunchbox at his side. He's going to work tonight. New Year's Eve. How many people work on New Year's Eve? I wonder.

The train stops at 59th Street and Columbus Circle. The car empties and refills with new blood, new faces to engage and avoid. A couple stands in the middle of the car, holding on to the center pole for balance. They sway back and forth with the train as it lurches forward from the station. Like a maypole, they use it to wind around each other, laughing and whispering as they play. They kiss and touch and talk with their eyes. I wish I were him. His hand is on her waist now, and so is mine. I tell her about the party, and she wants to go. She wants to be my girlfriend, and we take walks together in the park. I think I'm smiling and I stop, turning a page of the *Daily News* with my foot.

It seems like hours have passed. The couple left long ago. They got off at the Village. The man with the lunchbox changed trains at Chambers Street, and all the faces are new again. By now my foot has unraveled every page.

The train has left the tunnel and stops outdoors. A man enters with the morning edition of the *Tribune* under his arm. Behind him a group of kids enter, yelling joyously, "Happy New Year!" One has a party horn in his mouth, making those horrible noises. "Happy New Year 1958!" somewhere in Brooklyn. I leave the car and cross the platform. I lean on a battered gum machine and look for another train. The station is cold, warmed only by an occasional reveler. I think I'll head back now. My parents should be asleep by the time I get home.